AN OFFERING TO THE GODS

They were in blackness. But far off a flickering orange light crept through the trees. Not the sun, it was too low. The road curved toward the orange light, though. Blade kept silent and waited. They came out of the trees to an enormous ampitheater. In the middle a huge jet of brilliant orange flame soared a hundred feet into the air. Blade could easily hear the roar of the flame, and occasionally felt puffs of the heat on his skin.

Suddenly Blade knew that this was the Mouth of the Gods, a huge roaring flame—no doubt an ignited natural gas jet. He also knew what it meant to be thrust into the Mouth. A few seconds in the flame, and there would be nothing left of Richard Blade but a puff of greasy smoke and a few charred fragments of bone on the grill.

They were moving on toward the inner wall now. The towers of Kano were silhouetted against the blood-red sky. The beauty was gone from them. Instead they had a sinister look of giants waiting for death—Blade's death, or perhaps their own? He couldn't keep from thinking of the irony in his situation. Here he was in Kano, where he had hoped to come, to avoid dying in the heat of the desert. But here in Kano he might soon be burned to death in the Mouth of the Gods.

Quite literally, he had jumped out of the frying pan into the fire.

The Blade Series:

HEROIC FANTASY SERIES 21

BLADE
CHAMPION OF THE GODS
by Jeffrey Lord

PINNACLE BOOKS   NEW YORK CITY

BLADE #21: CHAMPION OF THE GODS

Copyright © 1976 by Lyle Kenyon Engel

All rights reserved, including the right to reproduce this book or portions thereof in any form.

An original Pinnacle Books edition, published for the first time anywhere.

ISBN: 0-523-00949-6

First printing, November 1976

Cover illustration by Ken Kelly

Printed in the United States of America

PINNACLE BOOKS, INC.
275 Madison Avenue
New York, N.Y. 10016

Dear Reader:

Adventure number twenty-one, *Champion of the Gods,* will mark the tenth year that I have been writing of Richard Blade's adventures to other dimensions.

I will never forget the day that my idea for Richard Blade evolved—a concept that has resulted in millions of sales and thousands of enthusiastic letters from fans all over the world.

It was in the office of George Glay, who was then Editor-in-Chief of Macfadden-Bartell Publications. I had always respected George not only for his editorial ability but for his willingness to listen to and accept new ideas for publication. New ideas, of course, were not sufficient by themselves—a writer had to be able to incorporate them into a manuscript that would hold the reader's interest from start to finish. I didn't know how George would react to my idea, but I was determined to try him.

"George," I said, "I want to do a series that incorporates science fiction, fantasy, intrigue, and history. I want to write about a hero who is England's top secret agent, and who is involved with an experimental computerlike device that is able to send him to other dimensions where he has thrilling adventures, such as those in *The Black Rose* or *The Saracen Blade.*"

George looked at me for a moment with eyes that considered the idea and rejected it at the same time. He said, "Jeffrey, it's hard enough to do a book in any of these areas, but to work with science fiction, history, and intelligence all at once is an almost impossible task. However, if you want to do an outline, I'll certainly consider it." In a week I had the outline on George's desk, and I was soon gratified to hear him say, "I'm sold. Let's go."

After eight successful Blade novels had been published, Macfadden-Bartell decided to cease their book publishing operations and go into the radio-television market. This left Blade without a publisher.

Andrew Ettinger, one of the most knowledgeable men in the publishing business and Editor-in-Chief of Pinnacle Books, had always liked the Richard Blade concept. He made me an excellent offer and he went on to develop the Blade series into one of the top selling series in the science fiction/heroic fantasy genre.

On behalf of Richard Blade and myself, I want to thank all our readers for the excellent support you have given us through the years, and to promise you that Richard Blade will continue to have even greater adventures in other dimensions to come.

Sincerely,
Jeffrey Lord
Canaan, New York 1976

Champion of the Gods

Chapter One

The man called J stood in the autumn rain at the Tower of London and waited for Richard Blade. A gray, wet, dismal day in London always made him feel particularly old. When he was waiting on a day when Richard would be taking a trip into Dimension X, he felt even older.

J's erect bearing and dignified manner hid a good part of his age from the casual observer. They didn't conceal it from himself. He was aware of every one of his years, more than forty of them devoted to a by-now legendary career in espionage. He had begun it behind German lines during the First World War. Like all spies who lived long enough, he was ending his career behind a desk, watching younger men go out to carry out his orders or die trying. The strain resulting from this could be concealed like his age, from casual observers, but not from himself.

Watching Richard Blade go out into the unknown was the greatest strain of all. J did not love any of the others like the son he'd never had. None of the other young men traveled so far, or faced such dangers with nothing but their own wits and muscles. None of the other young men were doing work so important for England.

Quite some time had now passed since the day Lord Leighton had wired Richard Blade's brain to a computer and sent him off into the somewhere called Dimension X. That somewhere had deserved the name then, and it still deserved it now. They didn't know all that much about it. There were times when everyone except Lord Leighton wondered if they ever would!

But they did know that an infinity of other worlds lay out there in Dimension X, each world with its own

1

knowledge, people, resources. If the day ever came when England could regularly tap that knowledge, those resources—well, perhaps the sun might rise on a new British Empire.

So time after time Blade went out into Dimension X. Each time he risked his life, each time he added a tiny bit of knowledge to the little they already had. Eventually they would learn the key to Dimension X or Richard Blade would not come back. No one knew which would happen first.

J turned away from that grim train of thought as Richard Blade appeared in the doorway. He moved toward J with that distinctive stride of his, a stride like a tiger on the prowl. Some secret agents could look like bookkeepers or refuse-lorry drivers. Richard, God help him, could never look too different from what he was—a superbly skilled man of action.

The two men shook hands. "I hear the psychiatrists have been giving you a particularly hard time," said J.

"I suppose you might say that," said Blade. "As usual, they seem to think there's something important about whether I bit my nails as a boy. And if I did, which hand did I bite more often, and which finger of that hand did I start with?"

J laughed and pressed the concealed button to summon the elevator up from Lord Leighton's secret research complex two hundred feet below. They stood in silence until the heavy bronze door to the shaft hissed open.

When they were safely out of earshot in the descending elevator, J spoke again. "They gave you a clean bill of health, though?" Damn it, that sounded like the question of a nervous old grandmother! But J knew he was always nervous when it came time for Richard to be shot off into nowhere. Since he didn't have anything to do now except sit and watch, he didn't even have to pretend to be calm. Not with Richard, at least.

"Oh, they did. My head's in the same shape as always, both inside and out. But they took a bloody long time to decide it! Frankly, it's a relief to be heading off into Dimension X again."

J smiled. "Leaving me to face the day-to-day routine?"

Blade had the grace to sound slightly embarrassed.

2

"Well, sir, you must admit you've always had the better head for administrative detail. I could never have done half of your job."

"No, Richard. You've always been the perfect and complete field man. You'll still be one, even when we find someone else to send into Dimension X and stick you behind a desk yourself."

"I wonder when that will be?"

"Getting tired, Richard?" J did his best to make it sound like a joke.

"Not precisely. But I must say I'll be a damned sight happier when the whole Project doesn't depend on me alone. I can cope with swords and slippery roads, but there's always such a thing as simply running out of luck."

That was a fact J had accepted long ago, but thinking about it never improved his mood. The Project *was* Richard, when all was said and done. No other living man could travel into Dimension X and return safely.

Without Richard, alive, sane, and ready to go, Lord Leighton's giant computer was so many millions of pounds' worth of useless components and circuitry. Nor would all of J's administrative work and all the Prime Minister's help for the Project have any purpose either, with Richard gone. Once more J uttered a silent prayer for just *one* other person to send into Dimension X.

But he had been praying for quite a while. So far nobody had turned up. He was beginning to wonder if anybody ever would.

Damn! He certainly was in a grim and gloomy mood today. He didn't need to look calm with Richard, but he jolly well owed it to the man to at least look more cheerful!

They walked from the elevator down an underground corridor leading through the whole complex to the computer rooms. Every step they took and every word they spoke was monitored by the electronic surveillance network that guarded the secrets of the complex and the Project. So far no one had learned those secrets and lived to carry them to hostile ears.

The first few computer rooms were packed with auxiliary equipment and the technicians to handle it. There

3

seemed to be more of both each time J came down here. One technician was certainly new—a tall, almost statuesque blond woman with a strong face that was handsome rather than pretty.

J saw that Blade was noticing the woman too. That was something else that didn't change, either. One couldn't say that Blade had a weakness of women, however. No woman ever affected his work in the slightest. In this as in so many other ways, Richard was both an English gentleman and a superb professional.

Lord Leighton met them at the door to the final room, the one holding the main computer. The scientist looked tired. J realized with a slight shock that this was only the third or fourth time Leighton had looked tired. Normally he bustled around in his filthy, once-white lab coat like some aging but still robust gnome. But he was more than eighty years old, his spine twisted by a hunched back, his legs twisted by the polio he'd had as a child. It was a minor miracle he hadn't been in his grave ten years ago.

The three men shook hands all around and passed through the last door. The room beyond was almost entirely filled with the vast gray crackle-finished masses of the main computer, rising to the rock ceiling and looming high over the men below. There was so little in this room that seemed made for human beings or even to human proportions! The computer consoles seemed like the images of strange gods in the crumbling temple of some forgotten and sinister religion. The metal-framed chair in its glass booth in the middle of the room seemed like an altar where Lord Leighton would shortly sacrifice Richard Blade to those gods.

J looked at Blade and smiled, amused at the workings of his own imagination. Richard, as usual, was as calm as if he had been preparing to step into a swimming pool for half an hour's brisk workout. Or if he was showing any emotion, it was anticipation, anticipation of what might be waiting for him in Dimension X. J knew that he himself had once gone off on field missions in much the same frame of mind. But those days were far behind him now.

J pulled out the folding spectator seat installed for his benefit on one wall and sat down. Blade had already

4

vanished into the changing booth. J leaned back as far as he could, wished he could light a cigar, and watched Leighton bustling about the room, making final checks on the computer.

A few minutes later Blade emerged from the changing booth, stripped to a loincloth and smeared from head to foot with a sticky, strong-smelling black grease. The grease was supposed to prevent electrical burns. The loincloth did absolutely nothing that anybody had ever been able to figure out. Blade always landed in Dimension X alive, sane, his head aching, and naked as a new born baby.

Blade sat down in the chair in the glass booth and Lord Leighton went to work. Like a gardener fastening vines in place, he fixed scores and hundreds of wires to every part of Blade's body. Each wire ended in a cobra-headed metal electrode taped to Blade's skin. When Leighton was finished, Blade reminded J of a statue—a statue in some city long abandoned to the jungle, now completely overgrown with a tangle of creepers and vines. As always, Blade sat perfectly still. With all the wires attached to him, he couldn't have fidgeted even if he'd wanted to.

As Lord Leighton moved over to the master control panel, I remembered to ask one of his usual questions. "Any tricks this time?"

"No. We're still accumulating data on Blade's return to Tharn."

J nodded, relieved. Lord Leighton was firmly determined to improve the Project in every possible way. So far all they could do was land a stark-naked Blade *somewhere* and bring him back with whatever he happened to be holding on to at the time. There was a lot more than that to be done if England was ever to benefit from all the millions of pounds poured into Project Dimension X.

So far, though, nothing they had done had broken the pattern. Once Blade had returned to a Dimension he'd visited before, the land of Tharn. But that had apparently been pure accident. Lord Leighton hated "accidents" with a violent passion, and sometimes he became a little too determined to prove the superiority of the scientific method. When that happened, he sometimes

5

threw novelties into the computer without consulting anybody else or even taking proper thought for Blade's safety. So far they had been very lucky. Richard himself had said that there was always such a thing as running out of luck, however. As he always did, J mentally crossed his fingers and prayed that this would not be the time.

The lights on the control panel showed that the computer was reaching the end of the main sequence. In a few seconds it would be ready to receive Lord Leighton's command to hurl Blade into Dimension X.

Lord Leighton reached out with one thin, twisted hand, in a surprisingly smooth and sure gesture. The long fingers closed on the red master switch. The scientist seemed to draw himself almost straight. This was his moment, the moment when the miracle he had made possible would take place again.

Lord Leighton pulled down on the switch. There was no sound, no thunderous roar to mark the power let loose, not even a faint hum or hiss. But a searing golden light flashed through the chamber. Every bit of metal and glass sparkled and glowed as if it had been dipped in molten gold.

J squeezed his eyes shut against the glare. When he opened them, the chair in the center of the room stood there in its glass booth—empty.

Chapter Two

It usually took a little while for Blade's senses to reorient themselves as Home Dimension faded out and Dimension X took shape. Usually he whirled through a nightmare of strange sounds and even stranger sights while this happened.

This time things were different. A hammering pain exploded in his head and a searing golden light swamped his vision, leaving him staring blindly into total darkness. Before he could even draw a breath he landed with a distinct and unmistakably real *thud* on a hard, lumpy surface.

The headache was much worse than usual. Even raising a hand sent pain stabbing sickeningly through his head. He felt nauseated, but he couldn't even gather the energy to retch. He lay still with his eyes closed until he felt the pain beginning to fade. A few minutes after that he was able to open his eyes, sit up, and then rise to his feet.

He was standing in the bottom of a shallow bowl formed by slopes of reddish-yellow sand and shiny jet-black gravel. The rim of the bowl was a series of undu-lating crests of wind-packed and wind-furrowed sand. Overhead a blazing sun made a cloudless blue sky seem almost luminous. Blade already felt the heat searing down on his naked skin. He licked his lips, which sud-denly felt a great deal drier than they should have.

Down in the bowl there was not a breath of wind blowing. Occasional wisps of sand whirling past over-head told of a strong breeze higher up. Blade started up the side of the bowl. Remembering his survival training, he moved slowly, to avoid working up a sweat that would cost his body precious water.

The rim of the bowl gave him a better view of the landscape. He turned his face away from the wind, to keep the sand out of his eyes, and shaded his eyes against the sun with one hand as he scanned his sur-roundings. He could see a long way in the clear desert air. For many miles all he could make out were humps, ridges, and more pits and bowls, mile after mile of life-less sun-scorched sand and gravel. The only thing mov-ing anywhere was an occasional dust devil.

Blade could already feel the furnace-hot, sand-laden wind blowing over him, invisibly but inevitably sucking the moisture out of him. How many miles of desert lay between him and human life in this Dimension? More important, how many miles lay between him and the nearest water?

Blade firmly reined in his curiosity. The deep desert was no place to indulge a desire to see what lay beyond the next hill. It was a place for one rule, and one rule only, for anyone who wanted to live as long as he could. *Make your water last as long as possible.* One way to do that was to not move by day—not a mile to see over the next ridge, not a single foot if you could help it.

Blade moved a hundred feet or so, to a patch of soft

7

sand in the lee of a small hump. He sat down and started digging himself in, working slowly to avoid getting sweaty or tired. A foot below the surface, the sand was thirty degrees cooler. Even a thin layer would keep the merciless sun from flaying the skin off his body.

In a few minutes Blade covered everything except his head and one arm. He worked the arm as deep into the sand as he could, closed his eyes, and did his best to go to sleep. He couldn't think of anything else to do.

The drop in temperature after the sun went down awoke Blade. He dug himself out from under the protecting sand, brushed himself off, and stood up. Taking refuge under the sand had helped. He felt thirsty, but well rested and not at all dehydrated.

Now he could walk without fear of the sun and the sand-laden wind trying to suck the moisture and the life from his body. The air was still and silent. Blade felt his skin puckering at the chill of the desert night. What seemed like a million bright and totally impersonal stars shone down from the sky. It was time to get moving.

He moved along swiftly, listening for any sound, looking for any light or movement. He saw nothing at all and heard nothing except the soft swish and crunch of his own bare feet on sand and gravel. This desert seemed as lifeless by night as it did by day. A good place to get out of as soon as possible.

An hour later he was climbing a ridgeline that marked the crest of a gigantic sand dune. He stood as close to the edge as he dared and watched the leeward face of the dune swoop down and away. The face plunged five hundred feet down, and long fingers of mounded sand stretched out half a mile or more into the desert. What lay beyond was swallowed in the darkness. No light shone, nothing moved. It was like looking into a bottomless pit lined with black velvet.

Blade's eyes scanned the visible face of the dune from left to right. Two-thirds of the way across he stopped and stood up, looking more carefully. Down in one of the little valleys between the sand mounds was a cluster of—things. Things that were unmistakably paler and sharper in outline than anything Blade had seen so far in this desert. Color and outline might be a trick played by shadows or overstrained eyes. They might also indicate something not of this desert.

Blade moved cautiously down the face of the dune, not wanting to risk starting a sandslide. He did not breathe easily until he felt under his feet the hard-packed level sand on top of one of the mounds. Then he turned and began scrambling along the fringes of the dune toward the valley where he had seen the shapes. Soon he stood at the head of the little valley, looking down onto the floor. The shadows here were deep, but they did not hide what lay below.

Bleached and frayed robes and the bones of men and animals lay scattered about on the sand. Some were half-buried, others lay as if they had just been dropped there by a casual wanderer. From one threadbare hood the empty eye sockets of a whitened skull stared up at Blade.

Blade stared back down at the skull. As silent as it was, it told him one welcome fact. This Dimension had human inhabitants.

This didn't surprise Blade. On all his trips into Dimension X he'd always found at least one people who were unmistakably human, whomever and whatever else he might find besides. Sooner or later he suspected he was going to wind up in a Dimension where the only intelligent race looked like birds or snakes or eight-foot turnips. He was perfectly happy to see that day postponed as long as possible.

There were a dozen or so complete human skeletons, the remains of several animals, plus assorted odd bones. The animal skeletons showed high arched backs, long necks, enormously long legs, and large splayed hooves for traveling across sand. Blade suspected the live animals would look remarkably like camels.

Blade knelt and examined the clothing of the dead men. It made him think of old pictures he had seen of Bedouin tribesmen. The basic garments were long flowing robes. Once they had been a dazzling white. Now they were faded and frayed, slashed and stained with their late wearers', blood.

Under the robes the riders had worn light tunics and trousers, and on their feet soft boots, now dried until

9

they were cracked, hard as wood, and quite unwearable. Blade wrapped his feet in rags instead. But he was able to find a wearable tunic, trousers, and a robe. In these salvaged clothes he would look like something risen from the grave, but he would at least have a layer of cloth between his skin and the sun and sand.

Blade next spent a long time searching for possible weapons, without any luck. He shook out every garment, picked up every bone, and nearly looked under every grain of sand in the area. Whatever weapons the dead riders had carried were long gone.

From the way the bodies of the men and their mounts lay, it was not hard to figure out what had happened. They had been moving fast, probably fleeing, certainly not watching where they were going. They had ridden into the little valley and had found that their mounts could not climb the slopes all around them. Before they could turn and ride out again, their pursuers had arrived and turned the little valley into a death trap. There had been a brief savage flurry of swords cleaving skulls and arrows and bullets sinking into flesh; then the undisturbed silence of the desert had returned. The victors had stripped the bodies of weapons and had left their victims lying where they had fallen. The sun, the sand-laden wind, and scavenging birds had stripped the flesh from the bones in a few days or weeks. Nothing was left as a monument to the dead except their whitening bones and the clothes now worn by a man not even of their world, let alone of their people.

Blade bent and picked up a pebble from the ground. He put it in his mouth and began rolling it around between his tongue and the roof of his mouth. The flow of saliva this started broke up the caked dryness in his mouth and eased his breathing. With his robe flapping about him as he moved, he strode off down the valley.

With the chill desert night around him, Blade felt free to move even faster. At first the great ridge of sand loomed high behind him, silhouetted against the sky and cutting off a vast slice of the stars. Then it slowly faded away in the darkness, and Blade could no longer make out any features of the landscape around him. He felt as though he were walking across the desert under a great inverted bowl that had him trapped here alone,

10

cut off from the rest of the world. It was an eerie sensation, and he wished again that he had a weapon of some sort. Even a dagger would have worked against the feeling that something might be lurking out there in the darkness, something against which all his skill and strength would be helpless.

Blade went on looking over his shoulder and listening for some sound other than his own footsteps all night. He also went on walking. The hours passed, and eventually the sky overhead began to turn gray, while the sky to the west began to show a faint tinge of pink. Blade began to breathe more easily as he started to get a clearer view of the land around him.

If any human beings had ever passed this way, they certainly hadn't left any trace of their passage. But at least this stretch of desert was not as lifeless as the one Blade had left behind. Here and there he saw small clumps of squat, gnarled bushes, with spiky black-green needles. Small mounds with dark holes in the tops suggested animal burrows, and once Blade saw the trail of a snake in a patch of fine sand. The sun had baked all the life out of this land.

It could still bake the life out of him if he was careless, though. It was definitely time for him to look for a halting place.

The land here was more rugged than it had been, and the horizon was closer. For all Blade could see there might be an oasis with cool water, date palms, and dancing girls just beyond that horizon. But if he couldn't see it, he wasn't going to risk walking by day on the chance of reaching it.

Instead he headed for a patch of bushes that spread out across the foot of a low ridge. When he reached the bushes he took off his robe and spread it out over several of the bushes. The spread-out robe made a patch of shade among the bushes. Blade lay down in the shade and began covering himself with sand again. Then he spat out the pebble that had kept his mouth from getting painfully dry.

Something about the way it glistened as it lay on the sand caught his eye. He reached out and picked it up, turning it over and over between thumb and forefinger. His eyes widened in surprise. Stripped of dust and

11

grime, the pebble was unmistakably black jade! That was a stone Blade knew well—his father's collection had been one of the finest in England. Unless he'd forgotten most of what he knew, the pebble was not only black jade, but black jade of the highest quality!

Blade sat bolt upright as he remembered all the patches of black gravel. Were they all pebbles of black jade too? Did this whole grim desert lie on a glistening black foundation?

Blade told himself firmly that the question would wait until night. He lay back down and covered himself with sand again. The question would not leave his mind at once, so it took him quite a while to get to sleep.

Chapter Three

What brought Blade awake in the darkness this time was not just the chill of the oncoming night. It was the sound of a battle.

Blade leaped to his feet as he realized what he was hearing. He snatched the robe from the bushes and pulled it on, then dropped on hands and knees to listen. In the still desert night sound could carry a long way, and in this rugged terrain it was hard to tell directions precisely. He could make out the squeals and screams of frightened or dying animals, human shouts, and occasionally what sounded like gunshots.

He found his feet itching to break into a run toward the battle. But he could only tell that the battle was going on somewhere off to the north. It would make no sense to go dashing off totally unarmed in the hope of finding a battle that might be over before he got there.

Wherever the battle was and whoever was fighting, it was short and sharp. Within a few minutes the noise died away. Silence returned, broken only by the skittering sound of a lizard hopping past Blade.

Blade was about to start walking north when he heard the sound of fast-moving hooves approaching from the same direction. He dropped under cover again and stared out across the desert, waiting patiently.

Moments later seven of the desert riders dashed into

sight around the side of a hill to the north. The animals they were riding looked exactly like camels, except for smoother coats and longer tails. All seven were moving so fast that the skirts of their robes fluttered out behind them like flags in a high wind. Several of the men carried short-barreled muskets with wide mouths, rather like blunderbusses. Others carried pistols or swords. All seven of them had bulging sacks slung across their saddles or hanging down on either side.

The seven pounded past Blade in an eerie silence, soundless except for the pounding hooves and heavy breathing of their mounts. The reek of hard-driven animals assured him that these were not ghosts, but he would have felt more comfortable hearing war cries or curses. None of the seven gave any sign of having seen Blade as they dashed past. He waited under cover until the last flicker of white and the last thudding of broad hooves on sand faded away to the south. Then he rose and began his delayed journey north.

Now that he knew enemies might be in the area, Blade moved more cautiously. He slipped from the cover of one hill to the cover of the next gulch, spending as little time as possible in the open. Every few minutes he stopped to listen. Silence had returned to the desert, as completely as if the battle and the seven riders had been a thousand miles away.

Blade kept the trail made by the riders in sight but stayed well to one side of it. So he saw and heard the fallen rider long before the other could have seen or heard him.

The man lay on his back on the sand, hands clasped over his groin, twisting slowly back and forth in obvious agony. Occasionally he let out a hissing moan. Scattered on the sand around him were a long-barreled pistol, a curved sword, and the loot from the torn sack lying beside his head. From where he watched, Blade could make out power flasks, smaller bags that might contain bullets, and several small vessels made of the black jade.

Certain that this man could do him no harm, Blade rose to his feet and strode down the slope.

"Jannah be praised," murmured the man as he saw Blade. "Now I shall die a clean death, and swiftly. I am all crushed within, my friend, so do not think there is anything you can do for me. Take my knife, and put it to my throat. Then Jannah give you a safe journey home, for those of Kane are sure to be out. They—" A spasm of total agony twisted the man's face into a grotesque mask. His jaw clamped shut so hard Blade heard teeth grinding.

Obviously the man took him for another tribesman. Just as obviously, the man was right about being mortally hurt. From the waist down his robe was soaked with blood, and both legs were twisted and smashed gruesomely out of shape. Probably his mount had stumbled and fallen on him, then had risen and walked off, leaving him to die.

There were a hundred questions Blade would have asked a healthy man or even one less seriously hurt. This man was dying, and dying in agony. He deserved what he was begging for. Blade bent down and drew the man's dagger from the blood-soaked sash. The man's eyes flickered upward and met Blade's; the pain-twisted mouth formed a faint smile.

"Jannah bless you and give you many sons, my brother. And when Kano is ours, may many of their women—ah, for the love of Jannah, strike!" as new pain tore through him. Blade raised the knife and struck downward, through the robe and between the ribs, expertly seeking out the heart. The man's body stiffened again, then relaxed for the last time. Blade gently pressed both eyelids shut, crossed the man's hands on his chest, and stood up.

Now there were weapons that the dead rider would never need again. Blade picked up the sword and swung it experimentally. It was about three feet long, with a heavy curved blade and a silver-mounted hilt, clearly at its best when swung from the back of a camel or a horse. If Blade had seen it in Home Dimension, he would have called it a scimitar. He stuck the sword and dagger as securely as he could in his sash.

The pistol was a long-barreled wheel lock that would have been nothing unusual in the seventeenth century. As old-fashioned as it was, that long barrel would make it formidably accurate at close ranges. It seemed to be loaded and working. Blade added it to his sash. Then he pulled the hood of the dead man's robe over the bearded face, turned, and once more headed north

He still kept the trail of the riders in sight, but was even more careful about keeping under cover The next man he met might not be helpless or dying. Or there might be thirty men instead of one any or all of them ready to shoot or slash first and ask questions afterward There was very little Blade did not know about staying alive while walking into the middle of a war That was one of the reasons why he was still alive.

Blade walked north in the desert silence for at least an hour. Once he thought he saw the silhouettes of riders on top of the next hill. A closed look showed him only a cluster of unusually tall bushes. their outlines twisted by shadows. Another time he found three carved jade figures of full-bodied women that had slipped from some rider's sack of loot. Otherwise he might have once again been moving across a desert that had always been empty and always would be.

Blade was beginning to wonder when the sky would start showing signs of dawn, when he heard a long, high-pitched, bubbling cry from beyond the next ridge It was answered by several more of the same. He stopped, then covered the last half mile in a slow, stalking crouch.

What he found was the scene of a massacre rather than a battle. The narrow valley below him offered good footing for heavily loaded pack camels. It also offered a perfect site for the ambush the white-robed riders had carried out with superb skill. At least twenty men in dark trousers and cloaks lay sprawled dead on the ground. There were enough detached arms, legs, and heads lying about to make it hard to count exactly. Thirty-odd pack camels lay among the men, throats laid open with scimitar slashes, their packs hastily stripped off and torn apart. A dozen or so more camels wandered aimlessly up and down the valley, calling to each other and occasionally nuzzling a body.

Blade scrambled down into the valley, sword in one hand and drawn and cocked pistol in the other. The closer he got, the worse things looked. Blade was hardened to grisly spectacles, but the sheer savagery of what had happened here impressed itself powerfully on

15

him. He did not wince or become sick to his stomach. He did find himself looking over his shoulder more often than before.

The way the bodies lay told Blade a good deal about the attackers' plans. Their first target had been the leaders and the rear guard, all of whom had been picked off in the first moment and perhaps by the first volley. Leaderless, panic-stricken, uncertain which way to turn, the caravan had stopped in its tracks. Then the riders had swept in to finish the work at close range with steel and lead, slashing and shooting at men too paralyzed with surprise and fear to either fight or flee. With the men down, the slaughter and looting of the pack animals began. It went on until the riders had taken all they were looking for, or at least all they could carry off.

They must have been looking for guns and ammunition, among other things. Not one of the dead had a gun by him. Pistols and powder horns were scattered around several torn packs. All had been smashed or cracked, as though the riders had been determined to make useless what they couldn't carry away with them.

Three of the robed desert riders lay dead among their victims, and two more and their mounts lay sprawled on the opposite side of the valley. They too had been stripped of their guns. The fight hadn't been completely one-sided. But Jannah's worshippers had still brought off a notable victory tonight.

Blade walked slowly up and down the valley, not quite sure what to do next, trying to look at the bodies as little as possible. Some of the shooting had been point-blank work with the heavy blunderbusses. Too many of the bodies had heads blasted to pulped bone and flesh, or chests and stomachs blown up and trailing bloody rags of internal organs across the sand.

This valley would be a paradise for the vultures and the insects when the sun rose.

By that time Blade knew he was going to be elsewhere. He moved up to the head of the line of bodies and began searching saddlebags, packs, and the belt-pouches of the corpses. Somewhere in this shambles there ought to be a map or something that would show him the road to Kano, wherever and whatever that was.

From what the dead man had said, it sounded like a city whose people were at war with the riders. It might not be the best place in this Dimension, but it certainly would do as a starting point.

Blade laid down sword and pistol as he searched, to leave both hands free. He kept them within easy reach at every moment, however. Every minute or two he stopped searching entirely, stood up, scanned both sides and both ends of the valley, and listened for any sound that was not of the desert. If anyone else had been drawn here by the sound of the battle, he wanted to see and hear him coming.

The first three bodies revealed nothing. Blade was just starting on the fourth when he saw several of the camels at the east end of the valley start to move. They lumbered up the valley toward him, breaking into a gallop as they went by. He snatched up his sword and pistol and dropped on hands and knees behind a dead camel.

The sound of the fleeing animals died away. Then the sound of fast-moving mounted men floated up the valley. Moments later a solid mass of horsemen came pounding into the valley and started up it toward Blade.

Chapter Four

Blade sprang to his feet and dashed for the side of the valley. The oncoming horsemen could not reach him up there without dismounting. They would also find it hard to shoot at him accurately, or in fact do much of anything else against him. That was quite all right with Blade.

Shouts rose from the horsemen as they spotted Blade. A few raised pistols and let off wild shots that couldn't have hit a sleeping elephant in broad daylight, let alone a running man in darkness. Only one of the bullets came close enough to Blade for him to even hear the whistle.

But the shadows that threw off the horsemen's aim also concealed the steepness of the valley's side. Too late Blade realized that the stretch he was aiming for was too

17

steep to climb fast enough. He swerved to the right, looked back over his shoulder. The leading horseman at least would be up with him before he could get off the valley floor.

Blade spun around, raising the pistol and sighting on the chest of the lead rider's horse. The man charged in fine romantic style, waving a long sword and shouting shrill, wordless war cries. Blade waited until the man closed within fifty yards, then pulled the trigger.

Instead of a bang there was a futile click, and then a sharp *spronnnnnggg* as the spring activating the wheel broke. Blade swore at the pistol, the man who had made it, all the man's ancestors and the man who was charging down on him.

When the rider was ten yards away Blade caught the pistol by the barrel and sent it whirling end over end at the rider's head. The rider dipped his head, making his lance point also dip. The point dipped too far and struck the ground. The lance whipped forward and up, and the rider catapulted out of the saddle with a very unromantic yell of fear. He landed with an even more unromantic thud almost at Blade's feet. The horse dashed on past, and Blade never did see what happened to it. He was too busy making his own dash for the valley wall.

He reached it before the next lancers came by. Blade saw one of them frantically trying to claw a pistol out of his sash, but his horse carried him on past before he could fire. Blade scrambled upward as fast as he could move in a half crouch. He wanted to stay low, but he wanted even more to get at least well hidden and hopefully clean away. Somewhere among those riders must be someone who wasn't hotheaded, clumsy, or stupid. Blade wanted to be a long way off before that man took charge of things.

Bullets spanged and fizzed off the rock around Blade as he climbed, but none came anywhere near him. He was halfway to the ridgeline before the people below realized that they could shoot more accurately if they stopped or at least slowed down. After that bullets started getting closer. Two or three hit close enough to spray hot bits of stone against Blade's hands and face. He crouched lower still and began an erratic zigzag course up the slope. It was frustrating to have to slow down now, when he must be just about out of effective range of those clumsy wheel locks. But he couldn't afford to give one of those clowns down below a chance to get lucky in his aim.

Now the ridgeline was only a few yards away. Blade had to fight the temptation to jump to his feet and make rude gestures at the men below. Another few feet—he rose from his crouch and took a long step forward.

It felt as though someone had slammed a bar of redhot iron across the back of his left leg, halfway between buttock and knee. Blade swore again in a blazing rage at his luck's running out *now*. He dropped to his hands and knees for a moment, then rose to crouch again, biting back a gasp of pain.

Below in the valley someone was finally shouting orders. Blade heard the sound of feet scrambling up the slope behind him, and, incredibly, the sound of a horse's hooves. He swore again. He knew he would never get clear now. He turned, drew his sword, and prepared to make a good last stand.

Half a dozen men were scrambling up the slope on foot after him, waving swords. Well out in front of them rode an enormously tall, incredibly lean figure on a thick-legged horse that he was somehow managing to get up the slope. The man had a sword and a pistol stuck in his belt, but in his free hand there was nothing except a heavy riding whip.

Blade stood up as the thin rider approached, raising his sword with both hands. He wanted to see how the thin man's grand gesture would look after his dead horse fell on him. This was one opponent at least whom Blade was determined to take with him.

As Blade took a painful step forward, the man's whip lashed out and down. Blade's wound slowed him just a little too much. The weighted tip of the whip caught him below the right elbow, stinging like a thousand wasps. Two feet of thin supple leather coiled itself around Blade's forearm like a hungry snake around a mouse. The thin man let go of the handle of his whip and vaulted lightly out of the saddle, drawing his sword as he did so. The light sword whirled down and then rose again in a lightning-fast arc, coming up under

19

Blade's scimitar. There was a sharp clang, and the scimitar flew ten feet into the air and landed with another clang.

Blade stood there, staring grimly into the thin man's face. He was fairly sure he was going to die, but he was damned if he was going to give this man any other satisfaction. The other had won just about fairly. So be it. Blade raised his head and waited for the other's sword to whistle in another arc, one that would end in his skull or throat.

It never did. Instead a shout came from below. "Ho, Mirdon! Wait! What of the Mouth of the Gods! It has not been fed since—"

Mirdon and Blade both turned and looked down toward the valley. Three more men were scrambling up the slope behind the line of swordsmen. The center figure wore a heavy cloak with embroidered edges and a heavy metal medallion on a chain around his neck. The medallion was in the shape of a leaping flame. He was the one calling out.

Mirdon turned back to Blade. The sword remained point-down on the ground, but the warrior grasped the handle of the whip.

"Ha, Rauf," he said, glaring at Blade. "You were not wise to come back to your kill, like a hungry jackal. Now we will have a little vengeance for those poor wretches down there. Where did your comrades go?" Blade was silent.

Mirdon dropped his sword, drew a small riding crop from his belt, and slashed Blade hard across the face. Like the whip, the riding crop had sharp metal tied into it. Blade managed not to flinch or make a sound, but he felt blood trickling where his cheek had been torn open. A pleasant customer, this Mirdon, at least to anyone he thought was one of the Raufi. No doubt that was the name the people of Kano used for their enemies, the white-robed worshippers of Jannah.

"I asked you a question, dirty Rauf. When Mirdon of Kano asks questions, Raufi give answers, sooner or later, whether they want to or not." He gestured with the riding crop toward Blade's groin.

"I am not dirty, nor am I a Rauf," said Blade in a

20

chill voice. "So do not be so sure that I will answer any of your questions."

Instead of another slash of the riding crop, Mirdon's answer to this was a great roaring burst of laughter. It was loud enough and long enough to echo up and down the valley. Blade looked at Mirdon, wondering if he faced a madman.

Eventually Mirdon stopped laughing and looked at Blade again. His eyes were not mad, but they were as chill, lifeless, and unfriendly as the desert night. So was his voice as he spoke.

"It would be better for you to be thought a Rauf than a liar or a coward. The Raufi are warriors, though it is their false god Jannah that makes them so. Liars and cowards are shunned by gods and men alike. They have no place among any people worthy of the name."

By this time the man with the cloak and the flame medallion was close enough to overhear Mirdon's words. "I told you to stay your sword, Mirdon. Did you not hear me?" The warrior's face set in an immobile mask. "It were better I thought you did not hear me. Otherwise it might be said you have disobeyed me. I am Second among the Consecrated of Kano, and in time I shall be First."

"In the gods' good time, this may be so."

"It shall be so," said the cloaked man. "It has been spoken to me, Jormin, in the flames of the Mouth of the Gods. Let no one doubt it."

"I do not doubt it."

"That is wise. Did you also hear me when I asked that this one be saved for the Mouth of the Gods?" His voice was laden with menace and tension. Blade looked at Jormin and found himself suddenly feeling much friendlier toward Mirdon. The warrior was harsh but not mad. This Jormin was at least a fanatic, if not a madman. The look in his eyes was unmistakable and frightening.

"No, Jormin, I did not hear you when you spoke the first time," said Mirdon. He spoke slowly, one reluctant word at a time, as though each one was pulled painfully out of him by his fear of the fanatical priest. "It was not my wish to disobey you, Jormin, for you are Second among the Consecrated." He said the last words in the

21

same tones he would have used to say, "Your mother weaned you on cameldung." Jormin did not notice.

Mirdon took a deep breath and went on. "But I ask you, Jormin. Is it wise to take him for the Mouth? I must ask him a few questions about where his comrades have gone. He is not likely to answer them without persuasion. If I must persuade him he is not likely to be healed in time to enter the Mouth as whole as he must be."

"No, that is true. Therefore he shall be mine, and mine only. You shall ask him nothing."

"But—" Mirdon's mouth opened, but only the one outraged word came out.

"Yes, Mirdon?" said the priest, his voice silky. "You seem to care more for your own victory than for the favor of the gods. I hope that is not so."

Mirdon's mouth clamped tightly shut. He looked like a man who dared not say a single word or move a single muscle, for fear of cursing or even of Jormin, striking him down. He stood, hard eyes fixed on the priest, for what seemed like many minutes. Then he let out his breath with a hiss and turned away. His arms rose, urging his swordsmen back and away.

"Enough, enough. The Second among the Consecrated has spoken. This man will go into the Mouth of the Gods. I doubt if he would have told us anything anyway, at least not until his comrades were all safely beyond our reach." Blade's ears caught in Mirdon's voice the tones of a man saying what has to be said, but not believing a word of it.

As Mirdon's swordsmen stepped back, Jormin's two bodyguards stepped forward carrying cords. They unwound the whip from Blade's arm and casually tossed it down into the dirt. They made him lie down while they cleaned, salved, and bandaged his wounds. They made him drink a strong fruit-flavored cordial from a silver flask. Finally they helped him to his feet and down the slope to the valley floor.

A camel was waiting there with a canvas litter slung on one side. Jormin and his bodyguards helped Blade into the litter, then mounted their own horses. The priest himself took the leading reins of Blade's beast.

There must have been a strong sleeping drug in the

cordial. By the time Mirdon and his warriors were mounted, Blade found himself drifting off to sleep. As the column moved out, one question remained flickering on the fringes of his mind. It went on flickering until he fell asleep.

What was the Mouth of the Gods?

Chapter Five

Blade awoke with sun glaring in his eyes and the sounds and smells of a camp all around him. He was bound hand and foot, and the heavily bandaged wound on his left leg hurt. He managed to twist himself around on his litter and get some sort of view of his surroundings.

The patrol from Kano was camped on top of a small hill with a view for miles in all directions. Flickers of movement far out on the red-brown sand indicated mounted sentries in position.

Several of the camels from the ambushed caravan were tethered near the foot of the hill. Their packs bulged grotesquely. As Blade watched, four horsemen rode up, leading two more loaded camels and carrying loaded sacks over their own saddles. Apparently Mirdon was salvaging as much gear as he could, but burying the bodies where they fell.

At this point someone noticed that Blade was awake. There was a shout, and the priest Jormin and one of his bodyguards came running over. Both went busily and silently to work examining Blade's wounds. They worked with so much pulling and tugging and probing that the wounds on both Blade's leg and his face started hurting him even more.

Eventually they stood up. "Good," said Jormin. "I thought the bullet was not in the wound, but last night I could not be sure. It has gone, and the wound will heal fast and clean."

"With your great arts helping it, that is certain," said the guard. Blade noticed Jormin did not look disgusted at the obsequious flattery. He merely nodded graciously, as if the guard had stated a self-evident truth.

Mirdon was passing close enough to hear the exchange. He did look disgusted, but only when his face was turned away from Jormin. The warrior's large dark eyes met Blade's briefly. Blade thought he saw sympathy, or at least curiosity, in those eyes. He also saw that Mirdon was indeed as tall as he had looked in the middle of last night's battle. The man stood at least six-and-a-half feet tall. He was also rail-thin, and Blade was quite sure he could break Mirdon in half without much trouble. He wasn't sure he'd want to, even if he had the chance. Mirdon was a soldier, a professional—or, at least, not a public menace like Jormin.

Breakfast was flat cakes of bread, cheese, onions, and sour wine with some sort of herb in it. The herb did not put Blade to sleep again. It did dull the pain of his wounds and of being moved around. He watched in a rather detached frame of mind as the men of the patrol loaded up everything, including him, and prepared to move out.

It took them three days to reach Kano. By the end of the first day they were definitely leaving the desert behind them. The bushes now rose nearly as high as trees, flocks of ash-gray birds flew overhead, and small herds of antelope ran off as the party rode by. Once they splashed through a few inches of slow-moving mud-brown water at the bottom of a gulley. They camped within sight of a small pond and filled their empty waterskins and bottles to the bulging point.

By noon of the second day they were completely out of the desert, into a region of small villages, sparse grain fields, and fruit orchards. It reminded Blade of parts of California he had seen when he had been in the United States for a desert-survival course.

Some of the villages and orchards were flourishing. From these Jormin's guards brought back whole baskets of oranges and lemons so plump and shiny they seemed to be glowing in the sunlight. From the sullen looks on the faces of the villagers, Blade doubted that Jormin had paid for the fruit.

This was also a frontier land, where the Raufi could strike at any time, sweeping in and out of the desert on their fast-striding camels. Wherever they struck, they left fields turned to dry, blowing dust, orchard of trees girdled, chopped down, or blackened by fire, and the ashes and rubble of huts and meeting halls. They carried the women off into the desert, slaughtered the men on the spot, and drove the survivors in panic into Kano.

Blade saw enough ruins and overheard enough grim-faced snatches of conversation to understand clearly what faced Kano and its people. For centuries the city had stood on the edge of the desert. Fields and orchards surrounded it, fed it, made it a pleasant place to live. But it had risen to power and wealth and beauty on the black jade. Blade had guessed right. Under the rock and sand of the desert lay black jade, endless miles of it. Five centuries of mining had barely scratched the surface. Another five might possibly make a real dent in the supply, if Kano lasted that long.

The black jade poured out of the mines. Some of it remained in Kano, to build the great beautiful city, to adorn its temples and its women. Most of it was loaded into caravans, into carts, into riverboats. The caravans and carts and boats took it off to all the lands that lay farther to the east and brought back whatever they produced that Kano wanted. Of all the cities known to the people of this Dimension, Kano was the richest, and all because of the black jade.

For just as many centuries, the Raufi had ridden out of their grim, sun-baked deserts on their raids. Their harsh life gave them enormous endurance and made them expert riders and expert shots. Few men of Kano could match them. Their fanatical worship of Jannah made them completely merciless and utterly contemptuous of death. They neither gave nor asked for quarter. They had always been formidable; they always would be. Over the centuries Kano had grown and flourished in spite of them. They had always been a nuisance, but seldom a menace.

Now, however, the situation was different. It had been changing for the last three years. A new war chief had come to power among the Raufi, a man called Dahrad Bin Saffar. A brilliant commander as well as a brave warrior, he had united all the Raufi as no man had done for three hundred years. No man had *ever* led the united tribes to such success against the men of Kano.

In the past three years the Raufi had become a menace—and one that grew daily.

It was not only the new united strength of the Raufi under Dahrad Bin Saffar that made them a menace. It was the weakness of Kano. No enemy had approached its walls in nearly a thousand years. There was a mobile fighting force, to meet the raids of the individual Raufi clans and tribes. That force was passably good—Mirdon was one of its officers—but it was small. It was much too small to face the united Raufi.

In the past, Kano would have hired mercenaries from lands farther east to meet such a crisis. Now there were none to be hired, at any price. Blade heard a good many bitter remarks about this. Had Kano been too proud and overbearing, until her neighbors and customers were happy to see her in trouble? Did the eastern cities and kingdoms hope to see Kano and the Raufi destroy each other—so that they could then take the jade mines and the orchards for themselves without effort?

The "whys" didn't really matter. What did matter was that the people of Kano now had to take up arms themselves. After centuries of indolent luxury, most of them were finding this painfully difficult. Even those who tried hardest found they could not learn all they needed as fast as they needed to learn it. The few trained men like Mirdon did their best, but they were spread thin.

So it was only very rarely that the men of Kano could meet the Raufi on anything like equal terms. Over the past three years they had lost five men for every Raufi warrior killed. Their strength and courage shrank as the Raufi grew bolder and bolder. It was only a matter of time before the Raufi had grown strong and bold enough to ride out of the desert in a united host and lay siege to Kano itself.

That would be final disaster. Fighting behind their own walls, the people of Kano might gain courage, but they would gain no skill. The Raufi might swarm over the walls and treat mighty Kano like any frontier village.

Even if the walls held at first, it would only delay the end. The Raufi would hold all the country around the city, the fields and the orchards, even the jade mines themselves. They would bar all the roads and rivers to reinforcements and supplies. If Dahrad Bin Saffar could hold his men together, sooner or later power and food would run out in the besieged city.

"Then the Raufi will dash out babies' brains on the walls of our temples. They will rape women under the bushes in the Gardens of Stam. They will stable their camels in the House of the Consecrated, and shovel camel dung into the Mouth of the Gods. It must not be!" That was Mirdon, in an unusual fit of passion.

Jormin's reply was cool. "We cannot hope to be saved without the favor of the gods. So it is proper that such a strong man as this Rauf prisoner be thrust into the Mouth. It is also proper that the words of the Consecrated be heeded."

Mirdon's face puckered up as though he had tasted a rotten lemon. "I have already said that I respect your decisions. There is no need for any more words on that."

"I say otherwise. You respect me when you are thinking clearly. But your wits are not always as keen as the edge of your sword, or as swift as your whip, or as sure as the feet of your horse. When they fall, you speak words best left unsaid. I must remind you of this." Mirdon took the lecture in silence, then spurred his horse on ahead, out of Blade's sight and hearing.

On the morning of the third day, they started out unusually early. By noon they had covered more than thirty miles. The roads underfoot were now broad and well kept, paved with a blackish cement and bordered with trees and bushes. Beyond the trees Blade began to see country estates, sprawling whitewashed houses roofed and trimmed with black jade tiles.

Another hour, and they were riding past marching columns of cavalry and infantry. Blade's professional eye took in their clumsiness, their exhaustion, the men who were barely staying in their saddles or on their feet. Only a few men here and there seemed to know what they were doing. What Blade saw now confirmed everything he had heard about the army Kano was improvising.

From time to time the road was half-blocked by enormous carts with six and eight wheels, drawn by teams of a dozen or more oxen or draft horses. On the heavily

27

timbered beds of the carts rose small mountains of jade blocks and slabs, on their way from the mines to the city. Each wagon was guarded by half a dozen mounted men, who sat their horses well and carried well-kept swords and pistols. They wore black cloaks, and a black pennant fluttered from a pole beside the driver of each cart.

The sight of the guards of the jade carts made Mirdon's face twist again. He spat into the dust, and Blade heard him clearly. "Damned Jade Masters! They think they can do anything as long as they have the jade. Even let us go down and make a peace with the Raufi, I'd bet! If we could get their men—" He shrugged and fell silent. The patrol and Blade moved on, along a road that became more and more crowded, through a day that became hotter and dustier as the hours passed.

It was nearly sunset before they came within sight of the towers of Kano. By that time Blade was sweaty, thirsty, tired, and sore in a good many places beside his face and his leg. He promptly forgot all his discomforts when he saw the city. The men of Kano had praised their city as beautiful, and they hadn't lied.

Fifty towers and spires rose high above the walls, some rising more than three hundred feet. Every tower, every bit of the wall, every building Blade could see was faced with polished, shimmering black jade. Some of the walls had patterns picked out on them in colored stones or polished metals. At least one building had a mosiac three stories high sprawling across the entire base of its crowning spire. Stones in a thousand different colors blazed in the mosaic, blazed so brilliantly that it seemed the mosaic must be made of jewels.

The approaches to the city were heavily planted with shrubs and stands of trees, and laced with small streams and ponds that reflected the setting sun. Short hump-backed bridges carried the road over the streams. At both ends of each bridge was a massive arch, tall enough to let even the high-piled jade carts pass under. The arches were covered with slabs of black jade, and the jade was worked into a thousand different plant and animal shapes. Blade saw a lion with jeweled eyes and the hair of the mane and tail picked out in silver, a dragon with gold wings and claws and emerald eyes, a serpent, an eagle—and on and on, until his mind couldn't absorb any more.

They passed through a gate in the outer wall that was practically a tunnel. The outer wall rose on a stone-faced mound of earth twenty feet high and a hundred feet wide. The wall itself was forty feet high and fifty feet thick, built of blocks of stone the size of small houses, every bit of it faced with black jade. The sun glinted on the helmets of guards marching back and forth on top. The muzzles of cannon poked out from ports in towers set every hundred yards.

Inside the outer wall lay the Gardens of Stam, several miles wide and completely encircling the city. Who or what Stam was or had been, Blade didn't know. What he did know was that a thousand years of loving work must have gone into the Gardens. They were a breathtaking sight.

Whole acres were planted with shrubs in full blossom, millions of white and red and yellow and purple blooms. The breeze was so heavily perfumed that Blade found himself coughing whenever he took a deep breath. It was like passing through a colossal greenhouse.

They entered a long avenue where the trees arched so far over the road that they threw it into blackness. From far away to the left a flickering orange light crept through the trees. Not the sun, it was too low. The road was curving toward the orange light. Blade kept silent and waited.

They came out of the trees suddenly, less than a mile from the inner wall. Here the road curved around the rim of an enormous amphitheater, half a mile wide and three hundred feet deep. The bottom was floored with still more black jade, and in the middle an enormous jet of brilliant orange flame soared a hundred feet into the air. Blade could easily hear the roar of the flame, and he occasionally felt puffs of the heat on his skin.

Around the flame stood several tall railed platforms and a strange-looking cart. It was an enormous grill of steel bars, twenty feet on a side, set on wheels ten feet high so that it could be rolled back and forth. Back and forth—into and out of the flames that roared up so fiercely.

Suddenly Blade knew what the Mouth of the Gods was. It was that huge roaring flame—no doubt an ignited natural gas jet. He also knew what it meant to be thrust into the Mouth. He would be bound to the grill of the cart, and the cart would be rolled forward. A few seconds in the flame, and there would be nothing left of Richard Blade but a puff of greasy smoke and a few charred fragments of bone on the grill.

They were moving on toward the inner wall now. The towers of Kano were silhouetted against the blood-red western sky. The beauty was gone from them. Instead they had a sinister look of giants waiting for death—Blade's death, or perhaps their own? He couldn't keep from thinking of the irony in his situation. Here he was in Kano, where he had hoped to come, to avoid dying in the heat of the desert. But here in Kano he might soon be burned to death in the Mouth of the Gods.

Quite literally, he had jumped out of the frying pan into the fire.

Chapter Six

The main prison of Kano lay just inside the inner wall. Here the streets were a tangled, cramped, gloomy labyrinth, winding endlessly among black, blind walls and lit by occasional torches in brackets. The only people abroad were parties of soldiers stalking about the streets and starting nervously at shadows and at each other. Twice the whole patrol was nearly brought down by a volley from trigger-happy guards. The shots and Mirdon's answering curses echoed through the silent streets.

The prison was one of those towers that had looked so graceful and beautiful from outside the city. The patrol dismounted, and Mirdon, Jormin, Jormin's guards, and four other soldiers formed a square around Blade. They headed toward a flight of stairs that led upward into the gloom.

Half an hour later they were still climbing. The inside of the prison tower was an endless madman's nightmare of stairs that rose and fell, ramps that wound up and down, corridors that seemed to head in all directions at once. Here and there were clusters of iron-barred doors with dark chambers showing beyond them. Pale, hollow-eyed figures crept out of the shadows inside to stare at Blade and his escort.

There weren't many guards, and they seemed to be poorly trained. But there never had been and never would be much need for them in this prison. How do you escape from a prison where you are certain to get hopelessly lost between your cell and the door? Blade wondered if in some distant corridors lay the bleaching skeletons of poor wretches who had gotten out of their cells, only to wander aimlessly until death caught up with them.

Eventually they reached a corridor where the view through the windows lay toward the outer wall of the city and the open country beyond. There were no bars on the windows, but bars weren't needed. It was at least a hundred and fifty feet straight down from the window sill, and there were a lot of hard rocks at the bottom. Anybody who got out that way wouldn't need a guard, only a coffin and a burial party.

At the end of the corridor was a large chamber, and in the opposite wall of that chamber there was a door with an enormous gilded relief of a leaping flame carved on it. Four armed guards and a woman sat on cushions just outside the door. The woman wore a short, low-cut blue and silver tunic.

"Ho, Arllona," said Mirdon. "I see you march forward in your career as a Free Prisoner. Now you can even dress as you please."

Arllona smiled. "Or as pleases the Prison Keeper. I am much in his confidence, now."

Mirdon laughed, a short, harsh laugh. "Or much in his bed. Well, I am not surprised. You had the soul of a whore when you served the Jade Masters. Doubtless you are now beyond the power of even the gods to change or improve you."

Arllona's expression did not change at all. Apparently she was beyond caring about insults. She was short, only a few inches over five feet, and so sturdily built that she looked almost heavy. Gleaming dark hair flowed halfway down her back, and her tunic showed off firm full breasts and well-turned legs.

Jormin's voice cut through the chamber. "Enough of this unseemliness." He stepped forward, half shoving Mirdon to one side, and faced the guards. "This Rauf was taken in the desert by Mirdon's patrol, in my presence. By my order he has been chosen to enter the Mouth of the Gods. He shall heal of his wounds, and then his time shall be decided."

Three of the chamber guards surrounded Blade while the fourth unlocked the flame-decorated door. A click, a grinding noise, and Blade was being hustled through an arched doorway into a large dim chamber beyond.

As the door swung closed behind him, Blade had a final view of the chamber. Mirdon was standing rigidly erect, hands clasped behind his back, trying not to glare at the calmly arrogant Jormin. The woman Arllona, on the other hand, was trying not to stare at Blade. Just as the door cut off his vision, he saw her eyes rise to meet his. Then the door thudded shut, and Blade was alone for the first time since his capture.

Blade was also alone most of the time for the next couple of weeks. He had visitors twice a day. One of Jormin's guards brought him his food, and a physician came to check the healing of his wounded leg and face.

The chamber where Blade was confined apparently dated from several centuries before, when a dozen people might feed the Mouth of the Gods in a single night. It was large enough to comfortably house twenty or thirty people.

The sacrificial victims were privileged characters, so the chamber was furnished with all the luxury that Kano's wealth could arrange. The floor and walls were mosaics, the ceiling gilded, the furniture massive, richly carved, and set with silver and jewels. Tapestries covered every patch of wall that wasn't covered with mosaics, and a delicately carved screen stood before the one window.

The screen could easily be folded aside to let in more light and air. Nothing else protected the window. A quick look told Blade that the window was quite useless as an escape route in any case. Below it lay a sheer drop of more than a hundred feet of smooth black wall falling to a roof garden far below. There was nothing in the chamber to make a hundred-foot rope strong enough to hold Blade's weight, and nothing to tie one to if he could make it.

Obviously, good treatment for the sacrificial victims didn't extend to making it easy for them to escape! Blade doubted that he had much chance of getting out of this chamber without help, or much chance of finding that help. Mirdon might not like his being in Jormin's hands, but the officer was just as determined to kill him as was the priest.

It looked like there was nothing to do but wait. He'd done it before and could do it again. Meanwhile, the food was good and his wounds were healing fast. He would be at his full strength and speed when they came to take him out of the chamber to the Mouth of the Gods. That was the one time Blade knew he would have a chance to escape, or at least take a few Kanoans with him as he went down.

Blade's window gave him a view clear out across the Gardens of Stam to the outer wall and the countryside beyond it. He could see many miles, out to where green fields and groves and yellow-brown hills met the luminous blue sky. The distance first blurred, then destroyed details. But he could easily see the glint of metal and the dust clouds as troops moved in and out of the city.

He could also see that the Raufi were striking harder and harder against Kano. Hardly a night went by without a distant spot of fire pulsing in the darkness. Hardly a dawn came without showing a thin pillar of smoke rising in the same place.

The strain on the Kanoans grew rapidly. The enforcement of the curfew grew more rigorous. By night the streets of the great city were as silent as a graveyard. Blade noticed that instead of six guards in the roof garden below his window, there were now four. A few days more, and there were only two. Blade wondered if the guards outside his door were also being taken away to reinforce the walls and the mounted patrols. Even if they were, it wouldn't help him much. Nothing lay beyond his door except the labyrinth of the prison. He would have to crack the secret of that labyrinth, then fight his way into the open past the guards at the main door.

So the waiting game would have to go on. It would not go on much longer, though. Every day the doctor nodded approvingly at the way Blade's wounds were healing. It was only a matter of time before he was a clean and unblemished sacrifice, fit for the Mouth of the Gods.

Chapter Seven

Blade awoke in darkness. He did not wake in silence. Softly, but unmistakably, a key was turning in the lock of the chamber door. Blade was instantly alert, but he lay motionless.

The faint metallic clicking continued. Whoever was trying to get in was obviously having a little trouble with the lock. For Jormin's guards or the doctor, the door always slipped open easily. Who else could be interested in entering the chamber, and at this time of night? Could Mirdon have decided to strike back at Jormin by striking down Blade? That would mean a deadly feud with the Consecrated; was Mirdon desperate enough for that?

More clicking, then a sharp, familiar *clink* as the bolt sprang clear. More metallic sounds—a key being withdrawn. Then Blade saw movement in the darkness as the chamber door opened.

The door opened slowly and silently. Whoever was pushing it hoped to sneak up on a sleeping Blade. At any time in any Dimension, that was something more easily hoped for than done. Blade continued to lie still, making his breathing regular and lowering his eyelids until he could just barely see.

Suddenly the door swung wide, with a faint creak of hinges. Blade saw clearly out into the chamber beyond. Pale moonlight and a dying torch showed that it was empty. The light also silhouetted a small figure standing motionless in the doorway. Blade caught a suggestion of long hair flowing down over square shoulders.

The figure moved forward, shutting the door behind

it, then stood still once more. Blade's ears picked up the faint rustle of fabric sliding over skin, the even fainter whisper of clothes landing on the floor. A moment of silence, then bare feet started across the floor toward him.

Blade was no longer tense. He saw that it was Arllona walking across the chamber toward him. Arllona, completely nude. Blade continued to lie still and watch admiringly as Arllona materialized out of the darkness.

Her body was full and abundant. But there was no excess to any of it, no flabbiness, no softness. Her magnificent breasts quivered gently, delicately, with each step. Her nipples were large, dark, perfectly centered. Her waist was surprisingly slim, so trim and neat that her breasts looked almost out of proportion. Her hips flared out widely, so that her gracefully curved legs looked almost too short. Her thighs cradled a perfect triangle of dark hair that seemed almost too bushy. Everything about this woman was "almost" out of proportion. Nothing really was, when you looked more closely. Somehow it all arranged itself in harmony, and the result was a robust, earthy beauty. Blade found his breath quickening in anticipation. As Arllona moved still closer, he saw that anticipation—or something—must be working in her too. Her lips were slightly parted, and her nipples had risen to firm points.

Arllona stopped a yard from Blade's sleeping pad and looked down at him. He could hear her breath coming faster, hear her swallow. She squatted down and reached out one hand. A long, sure finger traced a line from Blade's shoulder, down across his massive chest and flat, muscular belly, and stopped at the edge of the quilt. Gently, with thumb and forefinger, she drew the quilt back from Blade. Her other hand descended lightly, almost floating down, into Blade's groin.

That was the moment Blade chose to sit up.

Arllona went completely rigid with surprise and terror. Her eyes and mouth widened. She looked as if she were going to either faint or jump up and dash for the door.

Then she did try to jump up and out of reach. She also tried to scream. Blade's hands were too quick for her. One closed over her mouth, the other dropped on one bare shoulder, pushing her back down into a sitting position. He kept both hands in place until he felt Arllona's taut lips and tense muscles relaxing under them.

As Blade took his hands away, Arllona made a gurgling noise deep in her throat and sagged forward against him. He felt the solid ripe masses of her breasts against his skin. Her nipples were still solidly, boldly erect. If Arllona had been frightened, her fright was certainly passing away, and desire was still working strongly in her.

Blade raised both hands now, running them over Arllona's shoulders and down her back. With firm but gentle fingers he traced the line of her spine down to the cleft in her buttocks. He felt her arms going around him and her fingers doing the same gentle tracing on his skin. Desire began to bubble up rapidly in him too.

Suddenly the chamber seemed very warm. Blade kicked the quilt clear off the sleeping pad onto the floor. Arllona arched backward, stretching herself out on her back on the pad. As she drew back from Blade her fingers worked down between his legs. They did not linger there. Blade was fully aroused and fully ready without any more help from Arllona.

Arllona was ready too, Blade realized. Where she had found the desire that was making her whole body quiver, he didn't know or care. For now all he needed to do was meet and match her desire with his own.

Blade raised himself on his massive arms and hovered over Arllona. At first he teased her, holding himself high above her, only brushing the triangle of damp dark hair with his jutting erection. It took only a little of this before Arllona was murmuring incoherently deep in her throat, pleading to Blade to let her welcome him as he wanted to. A moment later Blade did what they now both so desperately wanted.

Inside Arllona was already hot, already wet. Together, she and Blade experienced the kind of snug, perfect fit the gods of love send to only one couple in a thousand. Nothing could have improved what Blade felt as he entered the woman under him. There is no improvement on perfection.

The feeling was mutual. Once again Arllona seemed

ready to scream. This time she clamped her own teeth firmly on her lower lip to stifle the sound, biting down until drops of blood showed. She took Blade into her in a silence broken only by a deep groan.

The silence didn't last. Two passions blazing so strongly could never have met in silence. Blade gasped as he felt Arllona thrusting her hips upward. She kept on arching her back and her hips until her buttocks were completely clear of the mat. Her breathing came faster and faster, harder and harder, until it seemed a continuous roar in Blade's ear. Nothing could bother him or distract him now as he plunged into the woman under him. He had reached a point where the prison tower could have burst into flames or the Raufi come swarming over the walls into the city without his noticing. He had reached a point where the center of the world was where he and Arllona were joined together.

Arllona's teeth clamped down on her lip again, to stifle a third scream. Her hands clamped tightly, clawing and pulling at Blade's hair. He didn't feel that pain. He felt nothing except the fierce spasms deep inside Arllona's body, the explosion that told him she had reached her climax.

Blade had not. He knew that the end for him was still far off. He kept moving as Arllona sagged down on the mat, every inch of her skin shimmering with sweat, her eyes closed and her damp hair tangled around her head. It was a moment before she realized that Blade was still strong, still deep within her, still thrusting. Then a broad grin spread across her face.

Arllona's legs rose, clamping tightly around Blade's waist. He found himself clamped as tightly outside as inside. Arllona—warm and solid and wet—was all around him, against him, drawing him in, holding him, imprisoning him in a new prison even more escape-proof than this tower.

The feeling heightened every one of the thousand sensations in Blade. It drove him onward, and the rhythm of his hips mounted steadily. Arllona's hips began to grind against him again, thrusting upward, twisting him from side to side in a totally maddening way.

The sensations and the madness could not go on for ever. They were too strong, stronger even than Blade.

He felt the fire rise in his groin, flicker, pulse, then burst out. A long groan tore its way out of Blade. His whole body jerked and twisted and thrashed desperately at the overpowering sensation of pouring himself into Arllona. For a moment it seemed that all the strength was going out of him along with the hot jetting.

Then Arllona reached her second climax. Blade could not have collapsed on top of the woman if he'd wanted to. She was moving too furiously in the grip of her own sensations. Her mouth was open, and if she had been able to scream at that moment nothing and nobody could have prevented her. But her throat was dry and nothing came out except a long fading hiss. Then her eyes rolled up in her head and she went limp, totally unconscious.

The sweat dripped off Blade and painful knots formed in the muscles of his arms. But he did not move until he felt Arllona beginning to stir under him and saw her eyes flicker open. Then he rolled off her, pulled the quilt over both of them, and put his arms around her. They lay like that for quite a while, until Blade felt he had enough breath back to speak, if not to move.

"You are here, Arllona. How and why?" He deliberately kept his tone and words harsh. He didn't want the woman to get any idea that the wild lovemaking had softened his temper or loosened his tongue.

The startled look on Arllona's face told Blade she must have been expecting just about that. She was silent for a moment. Then:

"There are no guards in the chamber outside. I have a key, one that I had made secretly for myself. I came here, hoping that we would do—exactly what we did." Blade saw a faint smile on her face in the darkness.

He reached out and lifted her chin until her eyes had to meet his. She tried to twist her head out of his grip, but he gently tightened his fingers. "Arllona, you do not have to risk entering this chamber to have a man. Mirdon said as much, the day I came here."

Arllona's face twisted with genuine anger. "Mirdon is a great warrior and a great mouth too. He does not know how I live. The Keeper of the Prison may not be a woman, but he is not much of a *man*. So why should I not—?"

"You still aren't telling the truth. Even if the Keeper was drooling and impotent, there are many men outside this chamber. There is only one inside it. *Why* did you come to the one—to me? Tell the truth this time, or I am going to tie you up and keep you here until morning comes and the guards return." He closed one hand around her left wrist to emphasize his words. "It was not wise of you to come here unarmed and then lie to me."

Arllona shivered in unmistakably genuine fear. "No, please, not—don't tell the guards. They will send me to the Mouth of the Gods with you if you do. I don't want to die that way! I don't!" She was biting her lip again, this time to keep from bursting into tears.

"Why should I care if you die in the flames or not? Don't tell me that this night should be enough, either. You'd be wasting your breath."

Arllona was silent for a long moment. Blade could hear her breathing returning slowly to normal, as she apparently reached a decision.

"I came because I can help you escape," she said at last.

Blade's expression and voice did not change. "How? Do you know the way out of this prison? If you do not, you know nothing I do not, and there is no reason I should trust you."

"I know the way as far down as the roof garden," she said firmly.

"But that is guarded," said Blade. He was testing her now.

"Not as well as it once was," said the woman. "I know there are only two guards there at night. That is still too many for me. I could not fight them. But they will not stand against a warrior of the Raufi."

"And then?"

"You mean, when you have slain the guards?"

"Yes."

"The garden is no more than the height of fifteen tall men above the ground. One side drops straight down the inner wall, into the Gardens of Stam. There are strong vines in the roof garden. Again, I could not cut them and make a rope of them, or climb down that rope without help. But a warrior of the Raufi—"

"You seem very ready to praise the warriors of the

Raufi, for a woman of Kano." Arllona was silent, but Blade saw something—surprise? alarm?—unmistakably flicker briefly in her eyes. His hands clamped on her jaw and wrist again. This time he did not hold back his strength. He wanted to frighten her, tear out of her the truth she still hadn't told.

"Tell me—*why* this praise for the Raufi? You are an agent of Dahrad Bin Saffar, aren't you? Tell me, then— why should I not tell Dahrad what a clumsy agent you are? I cannot imagine that he rewards foolish spies."

For a moment Blade thought he was going to have to knock Arllona unconscious to keep her from having hysterics. She writhed and heaved and struggled, trying to bite the hand he clamped over her mouth and pull free of the arm locked around her waist. She whimpered and gasped and moaned. Blade did not relax until she lay silent and still in his arms.

"Please," she murmured at last. "Please. Do not tell anyone. If Dahrad does not stake me out in the desert, the Jade Masters will do something even worse. I don't want to die. I don't!"

Blade reflected that she was certainly in the wrong profession if she was that afraid to die. Spying was a risky business in any Dimension. "You have my word that I will do everything I can to keep you alive, *if* you tell me the truth. Start with the Jade Masters."

It took quite a while to finally get the truth out of Arllona. She was no longer trying to conceal anything, but she was too sick with fright and worry to be very coherent.

The Jade Masters might be citizens of Kano, but they did not really care much who ruled it. What they wanted was the assurance that their lives, families, mines, and profits would stay intact through the worst the Raufi could do to the city. So the Council of the Jade Masters was secretly negotiating with Dahrad Bin Saffar.

"What are they promising?"

Apparently Arllona was telling the truth when she said she didn't know exactly. She was only a courtesan, once the mistress of one of the Council. By having her arrested on a minor charge, the Council had placed her in the prison. There she was to spy out the prison and spy on the Keeper. The Keeper came from an old and much-honored family, knew many secrets, and talked freely when in his cups or in his bed. There was very little that Arllona didn't know about making an old man talk freely, and very little of what he'd said over the past few months that she'd forgotten.

Now she had to get out of the prison, and soon. She had to get at least as far as the Gardens of Stam, where the Jade Masters had a hidden rendezvous for their spies. Until Blade appeared, she hadn't been able to even imagine how to make her escape.

"I have been in the roof garden. I know the way down there, and I tell the truth about the vines and the wall. I must have your help. Otherwise—" She shrugged helplessly.

Blade suspected that Arllona was actually a good deal less helpless than she pretended to be. But even if she was planning to lead him into a trap, it would take a strong trap to hold him if it caught him with a sword in his hand. Certainly he could not hope for any better chance to get out of this prison.

If worse came to worst, he would at least have a chance to take a few Kanoans with him, rather than to sizzle helplessly on that blasted cart! Also, the escape or death of his prize sacrifice would make the Second Consecrated Jormin very unhappy indeed. It was good to think about annoying that arrogant bastard!

"Why are you smiling so, brother?" Arllona asked.

Blade swiftly improvised an answer. "I was remembering how you came to me and what you had in mind."

Arllona laughed nervously. Blade suspected that in daylight he would have seen her blushing. "That was very foolish of me. I—I wanted a real man, not that old—! But you are a Raufi. I was fortunate that you wanted me."

"Why?"

"Well, you know, so many of you are great lovers of boys or other men. They will not lie with a woman except one they consider fit to bear their sons."

Blade's smile widened. "Well, you have seen that I do not think that way."

"Truly, you do—" The rest of her words vanished in a whimper of delighted surprise as Blade's arms went

41

around her and his lips pressed down on hers. Warmth and desire rose in him again, and as he tightened his grip he could feel it rising in her too.

Chapter Eight

The next morning Jormin himself came in with the guard who brought the food and the doctor who examined Blade's wounds. The priest hovered over the doctor until it was obvious that the man would have lost his temper if it hadn't been too dangerous to quarrel with one of the Consecrated.

"Is he healing?" Jormin asked. "When will he be healed? The wrath of the gods will be upon Kano if there is no one for the Mouth soon!"

"He is healing," replied the doctor. "Are you sure that the gods' wrath is not already upon us? The Raufi have never struck so close to the walls as they did last night. Do you think that you—?" He cut himself off as Jormin's eyes hardened. His eyes were murderous as they watched the priest turn away.

When he was alone, Blade went to the window and looked out. He saw at once what the doctor had meant. Not far beyond the outer walls, a solid mass of smoke a mile wide rose into the morning sky. Farther out, Blade could see clouds of dust and the glint of sun on armor and weapons as the army of Kano rushed about.

Blade realized that his fate now depended on the outcome of a three-way race. Would Arllona be able to arrange his escape before Jormin decided that he was ready to sacrifice him, or the Raufi swarmed over the walls? He and Arllona had agreed that the best time for the escape would be another night when the outer chamber was empty of guards. There would be no one to kill, meaning no bodies left lying about to give any warning.

But the guards' chamber would be empty only if there was another large Raufi attack, one that drew every man who could carry a weapon to the walls. The next time the Raufi came, however, might be the grand assault on the city itself.

"The very winds blowing off the desert bring the smell of the gathering of the Raufi," a guard had said.

At least Jormin would not be able to come secretly in the night and carry Blade off. He would have to warn the Prison Keeper, and if he warned that old man, Arllona would learn the secret. The Keeper would certainly mumble it in drunkenness or passion. Then Blade and Arllona would have to move at once, striking down however many guards they met—and hoping luck would be with them.

The days passed. Blade gradually took to staying up later and later, watching for the distant glare of flames that told of a Raufi attack. No one would notice anything amiss if he slept late in the morning. It was more important to be awake, alert, and ready to go when—and if—Arllona came. If Arllona didn't come, Jormin and his guards would, sooner or later. Then it would be even more important to be ready to fight. Blade didn't expect to survive such a fight, let alone escape. He was sure that he could at least spatter Jormin's brains all over the nearest wall.

Twice the Raufi attacked where Blade could see their fires. On a third night the sound of galloping horses and marching men told Blade of an attack on the other side of the city. Neither Jormin nor Arllona came, either by day or by night.

Again Blade awoke in darkness to hear the sound of someone at the door of his chamber. He wasted no time in cursing himself for having dozed off. Instantly awake, he rolled out of bed, snatched up the lid of the chamber pot, and padded softly toward the door.

This time the sound at the door was not the metallic clicking of a key. It was a series of solid thumps on the outside of the door. Blade flattened himself against the wall and listened. *Thump-thump—thump-thump—thump-thump*. Distinct pairs—Arllona's signal. Escape now—and prepare to face two guards.

The Kanoans were so sure that no one could get out of the great prison that they left Blade's door unlocked from the inside. As he slowly turned the big bronze wheel that freed the latch, he heard murmuring voices outside. Then he heard a wordless cry, unmistakably a

43

man's, and the thud of a body striking hard against a wall. At the same moment the latch clicked free. Blade jerked the door open just wide enough for him to pass through and strode forward.

One of the guards had Arllona backed against a wall. His trousers were down around his ankles and her tunic was up around her waist. He was lifting her clear of the ground as Blade appeared. The other guard stood by the entrance to the corridor, his sword drawn. Obviously he was supposed to be standing guard while his mate worked on Arllona. But his eyes were on the couple, not on the door. Neither man had a gun.

As Blade stepped out, the second guard's eyes flickered toward him. The man's head swiveled, his sword rose, his mouth opened to shout—all too late. Blade whirled on one foot and flung the chamber pot lid like a discus. It caught the guard squarely in his gaping mouth. His shout died in a strangled gasp and the sound of shattering bone and teeth. He dropped his sword and clawed at his mouth with both hands. He was still doing that as Blade crossed the chamber in three leaps and delivered a kick to the man's ribs. The smashed jaw sagged open permanently as the man crumpled to the floor.

Blade snatched the man's sword, then whirled to face the first guard. That gave the man time to drop Arllona and turn around. Blade shifted right, to get between the man and the entrance to the corridor. The guard looked at Blade's size, looked at the sword he was holding, and turned pale. There was only one thing he could still do. He took a deep breath and opened his mouth to shout.

Blade was too far away to grab the man, and the sword was too long for throwing. Arllona lurched to her feet behind the guard and clamped both hands around his throat. His shout died and he dropped his defense to jab backward with both elbows. Arllona doubled up and reeled back against the wall, fighting for breath.

Blade crossed the chamber before the guard could move again or try another shout. His sword whistled in a flat arc, shearing through the man's neck. Severed head and headless body fell to the floor with separate thuds. Spouting blood made a spreading lake on the floor and drenched Arllona. Fortunately she still hadn't got back the breath to scream.

Blade pulled her to her feet. He held her against him, tightly enough to calm her and also keep her silent, murmuring reassuring words in her ear.

Eventually she stopped shaking. Then she stripped off her tunic and pulled on the tunic of the first guard Blade had killed. It nearly reached her knees. Blade pulled on the dead man's trousers, which were almost large enough. Each picked up and belted on a sword. Blade pointed toward the corridor. "You lead. I'll follow."

Arllona headed down the corridor so fast that Blade had to catch up with her and slow her down with an arm on her shoulder. He didn't blame her for wanting to run. But running would be risky and exhausting. They needed to be quiet and save their strength. They would have to take it slowly, and never mind Arllona's jumping nerves!

They moved down the corridor and took the right-hand branch when it divided in two. Both moved with their swords in their hands. Blade could see that Arllona was no swordswoman. She held her weapon in such a manner that she was likely to chop herself in half rather than her opponent, if it came to a fight.

At first Blade tried to keep track of the endless windings and turnings of their path downward. After a while he gave up. Eventually he even lost track of time, so that he was slightly surprised when they came out in a wide hall. On the far side of the hall was an open arcade, with warm scented winds blowing freely through the arches. Beyond the arches Blade could see the loom of shrubs and small trees, and beyond that the stars in the open sky.

He put an arm around Arllona and briefly held her close against him. She responded warmly, her lips nuzzling his throat. He would have liked to say something, but the guards in the garden might be within earshot. He gently drew back from her and nodded toward the arcade. This time she followed him as they slipped out into the darkness.

Blade was sure he could overcome two or even four guards in the roof garden. He hoped that he and

Arllona could slip all the way across to the wall un-detected in the darkness and the thick foliage, without fighting anybody. If they found him the guards would die, but in dying they might alert comrades who could be waiting, armed and ready, at the bottom of the wall. If men with guns appeared while he or Arllona was dangling helplessly in mid-air, halfway down the wall—

They were halfway across the garden before Blade saw even one guard. He was only a helmeted silhouette, standing immobile, his face turned toward the sky. For all the attention he was paying to the garden, Blade and Arllona might have ridden past on horseback without his noticing them.

The Gardens of Stam were visible through the trees when Arllona stopped and put a hand on Blade's arm. She pointed at a long creeping vine that sprawled across the grass in front of them. She was about to speak, when Blade put a finger to his lips. She nodded as she also heard the sound of approaching footsteps.

The other guard was walking along the outer wall. As he came in sight, it was clear he was a good deal more alert than his comrade. He kept his back toward the wall and his eyes toward the garden, one hand close to the butt of a long-barreled pistol. He stepped a few paces closer, investigating the shadows under a bush, and Blade saw that the man was wearing a breastplate, a chain-mail loinguard, and a high-crested helmet.

That wasn't good. The armor would make it impossible to strike the guard down from a distance. It would be hard enough even to stab him before he could grab his pistol. One shot would give the alert, whether it hit anything or not. How to—?

The vine! Blade dropped on hands and knees and crawled back to where the vine trailed across the grass. It was as tough as Arllona had said. He drew his sword and sliced downward. He wound up having to saw through it a strand at a time. In a few minutes he had a five-foot section cut off and pruned of all leaves. He tied a knot in each end, to give himself a better grip. Then he returned to Arllona.

"Stay here, and the next time the guard passes that bush—" he pointed "—make a noise, as if you were sick. That will make him stop. I'll do the rest." He gripped

46

the vine with both hands and formed a loop to show what he meant. She nodded, face set and body rigid with tension.

Blade slipped away to his chosen position and waited. He would have only one chance. So far they had been astoundingly lucky. No one could have found the dead guards in the chamber above, or the alarm would long since have been up. One shot, though—

The guard's footsteps sounded again, soft thuds on the grass. Blade saw the silhouette of the guard's helmeted head appear over the top of the bush.

The guard took two more steps. Then Arllona moaned, a long, faint, whimpering moan, like an animal in pain. The guard stopped, standing in the open as he looked around, searching for the source of the noise. He was alert and aware, but not alert enough to catch the sound of three soft, rapid steps behind him.

Blade's looped vine rose, then descended over the guard's head and around his unprotected throat. Before the man could take another breath Blade jerked the loop tight. The heavy muscles of his arms stood out as he heaved up and back. The guard rose completely off the ground, as the vine tightened around his throat. His breath died, his eyes bulged, a swollen tongue crept out as his jaw sagged open. With a soft crunch the guard's windpipe caved in. He went limp and the pistol thudded to the grass from a lifeless hand.

Blade did not loosen the vine until he had dragged the dead guard under the bushes. Then he thrust the pistol into his belt and crept back to Arllona. A minute later they were both kneeling over the vine, slicing through the tough fibers.

They kept cutting and tying together lengths of vine until they had a rope more than a hundred feet long. Then Blade tied a large loop in one end, dragged the other end over to a stout tree near the edge of the garden, and tied the vine firmly around the trunk. Pulling with all his strength, Blade could barely make the tree shiver.

Either the other guard had fallen asleep, or he had taken their small noises to be normal night sounds. Blade carried the loop to the wall and helped Arllona place her feet in it.

"All right, now," he whispered. "Clasp your hands around the vine, as tightly as you can. Don't look down until you land. Then get out of sight *at once*. I'll be down as fast as I can."

He knew he would have to leave the vine-rope dangling, an open sign of their escape if anyone was looking for it. Even if anyone was, the dark green vine would not be easy to see at night. By dawn they should be safe in the hands of the Jade Masters, or even out of Kano altogether. So far Arllona had kept every promise she'd made. Blade hoped the Jade Masters would keep theirs, and he started to lower Arllona away and down.

He had lowered her barely twenty feet when a thunderstorm seemed to explode over the outer wall of the city. Six times in a few seconds, jets of yellow flame stabbed the darkness. Then the thunder of six heavy guns going off reached Blade's ears. The distant gunners fired a second salvo—and from below came Arllona's wild screams.

"The Raufi! The Raufi! They are coming against the walls! That is the signal! Oh, it is the end for Kano! It is the end for Kano! Oh, oh, ohhhhhhhh!" More cannon went off. The lights of torches and signal fires started springing to life all across the three miles of darkness in the Gardens of Stam.

Maybe it was the end of Kano, and maybe it wasn't. Blade was painfully sure that it was the end of any chance for a quiet, secret escape. Every Kanoan soldier within a mile must have heard Arllona's hysterical screams. Even if by some miracle nobody had heard Arllona and was running to find out what the noise meant, there would still be trouble. If the Raufii were really marching on the outer wall, the Gardens of Stam would be swarming with alarmed and hurrying Kanoan soldiers. They might arrest Blade and Arllona on general principles. They would certainly drive the agents of the Jade Masters away from the rendezvous. Within an hour or two, Kano would be tightly sealed.

Blade let out the rest of the vine as fast as he dared. A yelp of pain and surprise from below told him that Arllona had landed harder than she'd expected. He saw that she was on her feet and hobbling rapidly toward the nearest cover.

Blade had his hands on the vine and was about to swing himself over the wall when he heard footsteps behind him. He whirled, drawing his sword as the surviving guard dashed up. The man halted, surprised at Blade's formidable appearance and readiness for combat. That halt gave Blade his chance to attack, aiming a thrust at his opponent's throat.

The guard was a better swordsman than Blade had expected. Steel met steel with a clang that echoed around the garden. The guard disengaged with impressive speed and launched a furious attack of his own. Blade parried it, but not easily. The guard was nearly as big as he was and hitting nearly as hard.

Another flurry of blows. Blade was sure he could defeat this man, but that would take the time he didn't have! He drove his mind furiously, hammering out a strategy in seconds.

The guard launched another attack. Blade reached out farther than usual to parry it. The swords met with another echoing clang. Blade relaxed his grip and let the guard's sword beat his own out of his hand, sending it flying over the wall. The guard let out a roar of triumphant laughter and raised his sword for a downcut to split Blade's head open. Before the laugh died or the sword started down, Blade moved.

He lunged forward, his two hundred and ten pounds driving his shoulder into the man's armored chest. The man's breath exploded out of him as if he'd been hit with a sledgehammer. He heeled backward, eyes wide and gasping for breath. Somehow he found the strength to raise his sword again. Blade grabbed the raised sword arm, bending it until the elbow shattered, then jerked. The guard screamed in agony, then screamed again as he found himself hurtling forward toward the wall. A third scream began as he found himself in mid-air. Then it cut off abruptly with a thud and a crunch as he hit the ground ninety feet below.

Blade gripped the vine again and swung himself over the wall. He didn't bother looking down. If there were Kanoans already waiting down there he was a dead man anyway, and if there weren't he didn't need to waste time looking for them.

He went down the vine hand over hand. He would

49

have slid down, but the vine was so rough that sliding would have torn his hands to ribbons, leaving him unable to hold a sword.

Halfway down he swung his eyes upward. He was just in time to see three helmeted heads appear over the wall. A pistol flashed, but the bullet sailed off into the darkness unheard. Then something metal flashed high over one of the heads and came down. The vine jerked, slamming Blade painfully against the hard cold jade of the wall. The axe came down again, and the vine parted.

Blade had time to let out one yell of sheer, blazing rage at Kano and everybody in it. He knew he was falling, and he knew that his fall would make him an easy prey for the men who wanted to reduce him to a charred grease spot in the Mouth of the Gods.

Then the ground came up and hit him, and Richard Blade stopped knowing anything for a while.

Chapter Nine

No light shone in the chambers of the computer complex. The electronic monitors that kept watch didn't need any light, and no people were here tonight. There might be one or two night owls still working in the laboratories along the main corridor, but Katerina Shumilova hadn't seen any. Hopefully they hadn't seen her either, but even if they had, why should they be concerned? She was a computer technician, with every right and privilege to come and go in the computer complex when she pleased.

She was also a crack agent for the KGB, the Soviet secret police. Her presence here as a full-fledged member of the complex's staff was a major breakthrough for Soviet intelligence. She had been here three months. Tonight she was to bring off the first full-fledged act of sabotage against the "Project."

It would not destroy or disable anything that could not be repaired or replaced fairly quickly. Doing that would risk exposing herself to British counter-intelligence, throwing away all the time and effort involved in placing her here. The KGB preferred not to waste important and well-placed agents to win small victories.

No, what she would do tonight would simply cause temporary but spectacular and annoying damage. She would see what the other people on the Project did to repair that damage. She would listen very carefully to what they said. Everything she saw and heard would tell her more about the nature of the computers involved in the Project, and therefore more about the Project itself.

For all the time she had spent in the complex, she still knew practically nothing about the ultimate purpose of the Project. She knew a good deal, but all of it was fairly obvious.

The Project was vital to British security. She knew that simply from the size of the complex and the expense involved in building and equipping it. With British capitalism in its final agonies, the British would never pour tens of millions of pounds into something that wasn't expected to produce enormous returns.

The Project itself involved some major scientific breakthrough, and that breakthrough involved advanced computers. She knew that from even a casual look around the complex, and also from the fact that Lord Leighton appeared to be heavily involved in the Project. Leighton's reputation as a brilliant, innovative scientist, an absolute wizard with computers, was worldwide.

British intelligence was taking a hand in the Project. She knew that, or at least suspected it. She had seen the man known as J in the complex too often for there to be any other explanation. That was neither surprising nor mysterious. If the Project was as important as it seemed, of course British intelligence would be concerned with it. They would be fools not to be, and Katerina did not think British intelligence was foolish. Those Soviet agents who thought otherwise very seldom lived long enough to learn from their mistakes.

There *was* one unanswered question she'd found worth thinking about. What was Richard Blade's connection with the Project? It was an important one, considering how often he was mentioned in even the few documents she'd been able to examine. She'd also seen him in the complex twice. None of this told her very much.

She was familiar with the KGB's dossiers on Blade and on other top ranked British intelligence operatives. What she knew of Blade only deepened the mystery. He was a field man, a superb and formidable one with an almost legendary reputation. He was about the last man in British intelligence who would be assigned to *any* sort of desk job in connection with a research project.

She realized that it was time she stopped running her mind over ground she'd already covered many times. Somebody might still come in, and then there would certainly be delay, perhaps awkward questions. Ten years of training and field work had hammered a number of rules into her. One of them was: don't waste opportunities.

She unbuttoned the top two buttons of her laboratory coat and reached into the concealed pocket sewn into it just under her left breast. She drew out the doctored tape, checked the serial number, and double-checked the setting on the anti-tamper charge. Then she reached down and opened the lid of the main tape storage bin. She'd seen Lord Leighton do it a number of times, and her memory was superb. She could match every one of his motions as precisely as a ballet dancer.

The tapes already on the racks inside the bin gleamed faintly in the dim glow from the small light set in the lid. There was a space near the end of the second row from the top. Katerina took a firm grip on her tape and reached down toward the empty space.

If the computer rooms hadn't been soundproofed, her scream would have been heard all over the complex. The soft thud as she fell unconscious to the floor wouldn't have been heard more than a few feet away.

The signal did not awaken Lord Leighton, since he wasn't asleep. He was seated at the desk in the small room where he lived while Blade was in Dimension X. Being awake at three o'clock in the morning was nothing unusual for him. He seldom slept more than four hours a night. When a man is past eighty, he knows that he has only so many days' work left. Every hour spent sleeping is one that can't be put to some better use.

Then the desk lamp started flashing. Three shorts and a long, three shorts and a long, three shorts and a long—the letter V, over and over again. The lamp was hooked into the anti-sabotage devices built into several of the key elements of the computer system. Each element had its own code letter. The letter V meant the main tape file.

Leighton grinned. There was real pleasure in seeing his own work justifying itself. He had installed and wired in every one of those anti-sabotage devices with his own hands, working late at night and saying nothing to anybody. That was one certain way of keeping a secret—make sure it would die with you.

It occured to Leighton that few people might have suspected in any case. Few people realized how well he could still handle a spot welder or a circuit diagram. Of course, they didn't realize just how long he'd been at work, and what that meant.

Sixty years ago there had been fewer high-priced technicians around, and many more chances of electrocuting yourself in the average laboratory. He was one of the last survivors of that generation of scientists. He hadn't forgotten all the things he'd had to learn in order to do his early work.

He stood up, flicked off the light, and pulled on his coat. He had better go see what had happened. Then as an afterthought he reached into his desk drawer and pulled out the huge Webley revolver J had given him for a birthday present last year. Frankly, he thought it was rather primitive. He would have preferred a hand laser, and he hoped to live long enough to see them available. But he couldn't turn down a present from J, or neglect to keep it in working condition. Besides, the anti-sabotage devices might have really caught a saboteur, instead of having some sort of electronic fit. If that was the case, the gun might come in handy.

The device had been telling the truth. Lord Leighton realized that the moment he saw the white-coated figure sprawled facedown on the floor by the tape bin. He wasn't going to need the gun, though.

He knelt down, made sure the woman was still breathing normally, then opened the door to the main computer room, his own inner sanctum. Gritting his teeth at the pain in his back, he hauled the woman through the door. He kept on hauling until he reached the changing booth, then shoved the woman inside. She would not be very comfortable, but once he locked the door she could see and hear nothing. As for getting out, that would take a stick of dynamite.

Then Leighton pulled the observer seat down and collapsed on it for a moment. He hadn't exerted himself like that in months. Unfortunately, this was just the beginning of what looked like a long, tiring night.

After a few minutes he heaved himself to his feet and went to the telephone. Assuming that J slept at all while Blade was in Dimension X, he slept at his London flat. The scientist punched in the code for J's security phone and waited.

The conversation was brief, at least on Leighton's part.

"Hello, J? Leighton here. You remember I mentioned something about leaving a few mousetraps around the complex? Well, I've got a mouse, and I'd like your help with it. One of the lab technicians, a woman. Yes, full interrogation. So come loaded for bear. Sorry, didn't mean to imply that you're forgetting your business. Half an hour? Good. Come straight on into the main rooms. I've got her in the changing booth."

He hung up and sat back down. He would never have admitted it to J, now or at any other time, but he was glad to have the spymaster around and available. When things came to a head as they had now, J knew a great deal more than he did about what to do.

The clock showed just after five. On the surface far above them, London's early-morning life would be starting up. Here in the main computer room there was nothing but two tired men, one sleeping woman, a gigantic computer, and a knotty problem that involved all of them.

J finished resterilizing the hypodermic needle and put it away in the battered leather case that held his interrogation kit. He shook his head wearily. The last time he'd handled an interrogation personally, he'd been fifteen years younger. He looked down at the woman asleep on the blanket they'd spread on the tiled floor, and then at Lord Leighton.

"She'll sleep now for—how long?" asked the scientist.

"With this dosage, about four hours. I can give her up to six successive doses. We can keep her out until we've figured out what to do with her."

Leighton nodded. "I was hoping you'd say that. You know, she's a bit of a sticky problem."

J laughed. There was no humor or amusement in that laugh, however—only a great deal of bitter experience. "The logical thing to do would be ring up the Special Branch and MI 6. They can take her away and do further work on her much better than we can."

"Haven't we learned enough already?"

"Enough, yes," said J. "But not necessarily as much as she knows or as much as we could learn from several more days of interrogation. We can't tackle that without calling in more people and turning her over to them."

"Then why not do it?"

"Two reasons. One, she already knows more about the Project than any of our intelligence people do. Second, even if she didn't, we'd have to tell them a good deal in order for them to interrogate her effectively."

"So?"

"So that means a major breach of the security of Project Dimension X the minute we let her out of this room. A breach large enough so that sooner or later things that we don't want them to hear will get back to the opposition. At the very least they'll know we have Katerina. They may learn how much we know. They might even find out how much she knows. That isn't enough by itself to do us immediate damage. It is enough to make the KGB make the Project an even higher-priority target than it is already. That *could* do damage. The KGB is a formidable, tenacious, and ruthless opponent. I take them very seriously indeed."

"You don't seem to have much faith in our own intelligence people," said Leighton.

J started to flare angrily, then realized that Leighton hadn't meant to insult him. It was a sober scientist's question, and it deserved a sober scientific answer. He rubbed his eyes, which were beginning to smart with strain and fatigue, then spoke slowly.

"We do the best we can to keep our own organizations secure. But it is not humanly possible to guarantee one hundred-percent security against penetration by a first-class opposition. The KGB is first-class. It is almost a statistical certainty that there is a route to the opposition from inside the groups that would be interrogating Katerina.

"Besides, even if the opposition hasn't penetrated, what about our friends and allies? The CIA might not want to blow up the complex or kidnap you or assassinate Blade. But they might want—I believe the American phrase is 'a piece of the action'—for themselves and for the United States. Furthermore, if they know anything, we have to worry about *their* leaks as well as our own. The more people who know, the worse the problem gets, as I'm sure you've already realized. Your own mousetraps—"

J broke off as he realized that Lord Leighton wasn't listening to him. He was about to clear his throat to get Leighton's attention. Then he realized that the scientist was staring blank-faced at the ceiling, eyes half-closed and lips pursed, both hands clasped behind his back. It was one of the poses Lord Leighton adopted when he was working with total concentration on a particularly knotty problem.

Finally Leighton unclasped his hands and looked at J. "A question. Would we lose anything essential if Katerina were to disappear tonight, without any further interrogation, and without anyone else knowing what happened to her?"

J shook his head. "No. In fact, the opposition would have a nice knotty mystery on their hands if she just vanished. But how are we going to get her out of the—?" He broke off, as he saw Lord Leighton's eyes drift toward the glass booth in the center of the room—the glass booth from which Blade departed on his journeys to Dimension X. J's eyes met Leighton's. Each read agreement in the other's expression.

Why not? thought J. He couldn't imagine a more complete solution to the old problem of disposing of the body. There would be no blood or signs of a struggle—the woman would be alive and healthy until the moment Lord Leighton pulled down on the master switch. After that, Katerina would die more quickly than a good many people J had ordered killed, or killed with his own hands. He recalled a German colonel, dead these fifty years from a bayonet thrust into his stomach. There had been many others.

"Very good," he said.

Leighton nodded. "Do you have anything that will wake her up in a hurry?"

"Why? Can't we just strap her in as she is?"

Leighton shook his head. "Our information indicates that the computer won't operate reliably on an unconscious mind. She needs to be reasonably awake and alert, but cooperative. Can you prepare her that way?"

"Oh, certainly," said J. He opened his case, and as he did so an irresistibly amusing thought struck him. He straightened up with the ampoules and needle in his hand and looked at Leighton.

"I've just thought of something. Suppose our friend Katerina turns out to be our long-awaited new person? Suppose she can somehow travel into Dimension X and remain alive and sane?"

Lord Leighton looked pained. It was obvious that he thought J's remark in something less than the best taste.

Katerina knew that something unusual was going to happen to her. She suspected it was going to involve the computer that loomed so monstrously over her, and the glass booth in the center of the room. At least the two men standing over her showed no signs of taking her anywhere else, or calling anyone else to take her away. Also, they kept looking toward the booth and the metal chair inside it.

They had her full of drugs, drugs that kept her awake and aware but kept her from moving. In spite of everything, she was glad she was awake. She had been a candidate in physics at Moscow University before her KGB training began, and she still retained a scientist's curiosity. She would stay alert and observant until the end. She accepted that she would never leave this room alive, but she would at least satisfy her own curiosity if she couldn't do anything else.

That thought calmed her. A moment later her calm vanished, as the man she knew to be J bent down and calmly began undressing her. He worked quickly, not stopping until she was entirely nude. That in itself

57

didn't bother her so much. What did bother her was the way both J and Lord Leighton looked at her and touched her. She knew she was an attractive and desirable woman. Quite a few men had said so, and several had responded accordingly. These two were handling her as impersonally as if she was a side of frozen mutton, lifeless, sexless, and uninteresting.

It was even worse when they began smearing the black cream on her skin. It smelled dreadful, and they were smearing it on in great dripping, gooey handfuls. They were touching every inch of her skin, even smearing the stuff into her pubic hair. But they were still doing it impersonally. Now they reminded her of two mechanics hard at work on an automobile.

They lifted her, carried her over to the booth, and sat her down in the chair. The seat was made of black rubber that felt unpleasantly cold against her bare skin. Lord Leighton went to work, attaching an incredible number of electrodes to every part of her body. From each electrode a wire ran off into the computer. Leighton's touch and manner remained as lifeless as the computer, even when he attached an electrode to each of her nipples.

Eventually Lord Leighton ran out of electrodes, or at least of places on her body to attach them. Lights were flashing on the computer's main console. Now it was obviously programmed and ready for—whatever was about to happen. Katerina found herself wanting to hold her breath, forced herself not to, but could not make herself relax. In another few moments she would know the secret of this Project, a mightier secret than any Soviet agent or scientist had ever unearthed. A moment after that she would be dead, but she would be dead *knowing,* rather than ignorant. Somehow that was enormously important to her.

The two men were standing side by side in front of the main console now. Both of them were looking at her, but Lord Leighton's hand was resting on the plastic handle of a large red switch. His fingers closed on the handle and began to pull the switch downward in its slot. It reached the bottom, and Katerina's world exploded.

It felt as though a giant hand with steel fingers ending

58

in red-hot claws had clamped down on her head, squeezing and squeezing until her skull cracked and her brains ran out and were charred by the claws. She had never felt such pain, never even imagined that she could feel such pain. Then another giant hand clamped itself just as tightly on her stomach and groin.

She screamed then, screamed in pain, screamed in fear, screamed at the sense of loss that filled her. She was going to die without knowing what the Project was all about, die in agony, die with her body bursting open like a rotten fruit and melting like butter in the sun. She screamed as if by screaming loudly enough she could forget the pain or drive it away. She screamed, and screamed, and screamed—

Chapter Ten

Blade awoke and soon realized that he was tied hand and foot to some sort of framework. He could feel the ropes around his wrists and ankles, and hard rods digging into his back and thighs. He was quite effectively immobilized.

It took him a while to realize that he hadn't broken any bones or smashed up anything inside in falling nearly forty feet. He had certainly picked up a lovely collection of bruises on every bit of skin he could see, and aches and pains in every joint he could feel. However, he had felt much worse on other occasions and still been able to move, run, and fight.

Blade raised his head as far as he could and looked around. Twenty feet away Arllona lay spread-eagled, naked on a wooden frame. On her forehead someone had painted or tattooed the flame emblem of the Consecrated. Her eyes were closed, but Blade could see the slow, regular rise and fall of her breasts. He hoped she would stay unconscious. After all the poor woman had been through, the least she deserved was to die without any more terror or pain.

Beyond Arllona rose a stand of tall trees. Through the trees Blade saw the orange glow of the Mouth of the Gods, blanking out about a third of the stars overhead.

Listening carefully, Blade could hear the roar as the great jet of ignited gas leaped into the sky.

He could also hear, not so faintly, another sound. Not far away heavy cannon were going off in irregular salvos. In the intervals of silence Blade could hear the faint sound of musketry. The firing seemed to be coming from the outer walls. The Raufi must have settled down within range. At least they were not over the outer wall—yet.

Twenty-odd men were standing on the fringes of the trees. About half of them were soldiers. In the glow from the Mouth Blade saw that their faces were chalk colored with fear and slick with sweat. The others wore the robes of the Consecrated. Standing among them was Jormin. From the way he was waving his arms, he appeared to Blade to be making some sort of impassioned speech. His sleeves flapped like the wings of a drunken bird as he spoke. Blade couldn't hear a single word, but he doubted that he was missing very much.

Blade made another test of his bonds. They were not only well tied, they felt like wire, or something similar that would not burn, chafe, or cut. That made his chances of escaping before they thrust him into the Mouth of the Gods even smaller than before.

Blade calmly faced the vision of himself dissolving in the flames until there was nothing left but charred bone and grease, then put it firmly out of his mind. He slowed his breathing and settled down to gather as much strength as he could. His chances of escaping looked very slim. His chances of taking a few Kanoans with him and dying a quicker and cleaner death than the one awaiting him in the Mouth of the Gods—that was something else. He wanted to be ready.

After a while Jormin's speech came to an end. Either he'd run out of things to say or his audience had run out of patience. Jormin led the rest of the Consecrated over toward Arllona. Blade got a good look at their faces as they stood around her, looking down. The ugliness of frustrated lust was on every one of those faces. The Consecrated were sworn to celibacy and asceticism, but those faces told a very different story. One or two of the robed men were bold enough to bend down and stroke Arllona's unresisting flesh with red-gloved hands.

Jormin finally called his group to order and led them toward Blade. Blade started thinking of particularly ripe insults to throw at Jormin. The priest stalked closer, his face drained of all emotion except triumph.

Then three deep-toned trumpets sounded from behind Blade, loud enough to drown out the Mouth of the Gods and the distant gunfire. Jormin's head jerked up as if it had been pulled by a noose. A moment later the trumpets sounded again, and after that came the thud of several sets of hooves and many pairs of fast-moving feet. Jormin's head swung to the right and the look of triumph vanished from his face like a puff of smoke.

Three men in the uniforms of the lay servants of the Consecrated rode into view, mounted on three barrel-chested black horses. Each man carried a silver trumpet. They reined to a stop with practiced ease, put the trumpets to their lips, and blew again. Jormin's face twisted. He looked as though he wanted to burst into tears, or into a fit of temper, or into both at once. Then, slowly, with obvious reluctance, he went down on both knees. The other Consecrated did the same, and so did the soldiers under the trees. All faced in the direction from which the riders had come.

The sound of running feet grew louder. Then a dozen armed lay servants came into view. Behind them ran twelve powerfully built slaves, naked except for black loincloths. They carried a large closed sedan chair of heavily carved and gilded wood, with black jade panels and silver flame ornaments set into the doors. They stopped between Blade and the three horsemen, who dismounted and blew their trumpets once more. All eyes shifted to the sedan chair. The door facing Blade opened on noiseless silver hinges, and a man stepped out.

Not just a man, Blade realized. A man of *power*. He wore the robes of one of the Consecrated, with a deep border of purple, red, and silver embroidery, snugly belted in by a broad green belt with a flame-shaped gold buckle set with rubies. From the belt hung a silver-sheathed dagger and a gilded leather purse.

The staff the man held out in front of him quickly

drew Blade's eyes away from the robes. It was a simple design—a four-foot cylinder of black jade about three inches in diameter. But every square inch of its surface was carved with gilded flame shapes or covered by silver rings set with rubies and emeralds. Around one end was a circle of sapphires, on the other an enormous diamond of at least a thousand carats.

Eye-dazzling fire in a dozen colors glinted from the staff as the priest raised it over his head. His thin arms easily held it there for a moment, then lowered it to waist level. Jarmin hesitated briefly, then dashed forward so fast that he nearly stumbled and sprawled on his face in front of the man. He recovered, went to his knees, and held out his hands for the staff. The new man stared down at Jormin with a totally blank face that somehow conveyed a more searing contempt than any glare. Then, slowly, he lowered the staff into Jormin's hands and crossed his arms on his chest. Jormin backed away without speaking or even rising to his feet.

The new man would not have needed his staff or robes to convey the impression of power and authority. Blade realized that the man could have done just as well if he'd been wearing no more than a slave's loincloth. He stood well over six feet tall, with much the same lean build and long bony face as Mirdon. He was entirely bald, and his deep-set eyes roamed about continuously. In another man that might have suggested nervousness. In this man it suggested that nothing escaped his attention or his judgment. It reduced the rest of the Consecrated, even Jormin, to a collection of guilty schoolboys waiting for the teacher to hand out punishments.

The silence went on and on, until finally the tall man spoke.

"Jormin, you considered that my Meditation gave you the right to act as you have?"

"It cannot be that you would wish no one to enter the Mouth of the Gods, even at a time like this, when the—"

"I know what the time is, Jormin. It cannot be that you know my mind. It also cannot be that this which you have done is pleasing to me."

Jormin turned even paler at those words. Whatever he had been about to say died in his throat with a gurgle. He now looked less like a schoolboy than like a prisoner waiting for sentence to be pronounced by a notoriously severe judge. Blade had a momentary and delightful vision—Jormin, spread-eagled on another rack and being thrust into the Mouth of the Gods along with himself and Arllona.

Again the tall man let the silence drag on, apparently just to make Jormin nervous. Blade sighed. He was more or less resigned to dying. He was not resigned to enduring several hours of ceremonies, speeches, and religious politics beforehand. Besides, the longer the Consecrated went on blathering, the more likely Arllona would be to wake up. Then she would not only have to die, but to die in panic and agony.

Finally the tall man spoke. "It is not pleasing. You, Jormin, are not First among the Consecrated. I, Tyan, am First. I am First even during Meditation. I will be First until *I* choose to be so no longer, or the gods themselves call me to judgment. It is understandable, Jormin, that you forgot that. You always found it difficult to remember your place among the Consecrated. That was true when you were only Ninth among the Scholars; it is true today. It is not pleasing." Jormin, Blade noticed, looked about ready to fall over in a dead faint. Blade hoped he would.

"But you have done nothing against the laws of Kano or of the gods. You sought to make a proper sacrifice, although you also sought glory for youself. Indeed, a proper sacrifice is needed at this time. So you have shown zeal proper to one of the Consecrated.

"There are questions to be asked, as to how this man and this woman came to escape from the prison. I shall not ask them of you, Jormin, nor of anyone here and now."

Tyan strode forward until he stood between Blade and Arllona. He raised both hands high, then pointed one at Blade and the other at the woman. "I, Tyan, declare that these sacrifices have been prepared fitly, according to all that governs these preparations. I, Tyan, declare that neither bears a blemish that makes them unfit for the Mouth of the Gods. I, Tyan, First Consecrated of the Gods of Kano, bid the sacrifice proceed as it has begun!"

The last sentence rang out across the clearing like another trumpet call. Jormin straightened up, looking like a man reprieved from death. The other Consecrated and the soldiers started off in various directions.

"Hold!" Tyan's voice thundered out again. "One more order I shall give. Let Commander Mirdon be summoned from wherever he is, with such soldiers of Kano as he chooses to accompany him."

Jormin turned to stare at his superior. His eyes were wide, and his mouth was working with anger that seemed about ready to explode into total defiance. With an obvious effort he kept his voice level.

"Commander Mirdon is doubtless at his post upon the walls. Do you wish him summoned even from there?"

"Yes," said Tyan coolly. "It will educate you, Jormin, to have Mirdon be the Guard for this sacrifice at the Mouth of the Gods."

Jormin's eyes blazed, then once more he controlled himself and turned away, shoulders slumping. Obviously it enraged Jormin to have his enemy Mirdon given what was presumably a high honor.

It was hard to see that it mattered very much, though. Mirdon would be honored, Jormin humiliated. He Richard Blade, would almost certainly be dead within two hours.

The slaves, the soldiers, and the Consecrated—obviously had carried out dozens of sacrifices. They knew what to do and did it rapidly, efficiently, and without giving Blade any chance for a single move of his own.

Unfortunately Arllona had time to wake up. She screamed when she did, writhing and twisting against her bonds. She went on screaming and writhing until two of the Consecrated jammed a gag into her mouth and wrapped her wrists and ankles so they wouldn't chafe or scrape. Then she could only lie, panting, quivering, her eyes staring wildly like a trapped animal's.

More than the soldiers and the Consecrated, it was Arllona who kept Blade from making a move on his own. Several times he could have struck out or even made a run for it. He would undoubtedly have died a quicker death than he was going to in the Mouth of the Gods. But he would have left Arllona to face the Mouth

64

by herself. Blade was willing to endure the slower death of the Mouth so that Arllona did not have to die alone.

They were carried swiftly on their grates to the huge metal cart and raised to the broad grill on top. They were placed side by side there, held in place by heavy metal bands around their waists and ankles. It did not make any difference that their hands were free—it would have taken a blowtorch to cut through any of the bands.

Blade wondered if they would be drugged beforehand, but they were given nothing, not even water. He licked his dry lips and listened to the remarks of the soldiers and the Consecrated. Apparently the writhings and the screams of the victims were part of the sacrifice. He hoped Arllona didn't realize that.

The cart was more than a hundred feet from the flames of the Mouth, but Blade could already feel its heat against his skin. The cart stood there, while Consecrated and soldiers dashed about like busy ants, doing a hundred and one last-minute things.

Mirdon rode up, sprang down from his horse, strode across the gleaming jade blocks of the pit to where Tyan stood waiting. They greeted each other with elaborately ceremonial courtesy, then, side by side, mounted the steps to the stand nearest the Mouth. Tyan was carrying his great staff; the reflections from the gold and the jewels made it look like a bar of solid fire. As Tyan and Mirdon took their places, all movement in the pit ceased.

A score of soldiers ran forward, carrying a T-shaped metal bar twenty feet long. They pushed the foot of the T into a socket in the rear of the cart, took positions along the crossbar, and began to shove. Blade noted with an almost detached interest this solution to the problem of pushing the cart into the Mouth without the pushers being burned up along with the sacrifice.

The cart moved forward slowly, jerkily, with many rattles and clanks. One wheel had a distinctive sound, a sort of *brrraaaank!* Blade counted carefully. Each time the wheel sounded meant ten feet closer to the Mouth.

Eighty feet to go. The heat was stronger now. It would be uncomfortable at seventy, painful at fifty, unendurable at forty. They would both probably be unconscious before any real flame touched them. That was a hopeful thought, now.

Seventy feet. It *was* getting uncomfortable. The bands and the bars of the grill were beginning to warm up as the heat came in waves from the Mouth. Blade looked at Arllona. She lay totally rigid, her lips showing drops of blood where she'd bitten them. Her eyes rolled toward him and met his.

Sixty feet. The light and the heat from the soaring column of flame that was the Mouth of the Gods poured over him, shutting out the world. He could no longer hear the wheels to measure their advance toward the Mouth. He could no longer hear anything except the steadily growing roar of the flames.

Fifty feet. There was pain now, pain over every inch of skin, more pain where the hot metal touched him. He could hear Arllona screaming now. He forced himself to go on taking shallow, regular breaths. In another moment the air would be hot enough to burn out his lungs. Then his own self-control might snap as thoroughly as Arllona's, and he would be screaming too, and—

Blade gasped, coughed as he inhaled scorching air, and sat up. There was a new pain now, an agonizing, stabbing pain in his head—a new pain, but also a familiar one. Somehow the computer had reached out for him, somehow it was gripping his brain now, to snatch him away from here, snatch him back to Home Dimension—

—and snatch Arllona too! It was worth a try, even if—! Blade didn't take time to complete the thought. Instead he twisted around as far as he could, laying one hand on Arllona's forehead and another over her wildly beating heart. She was alternately screaming and gibbering hysterically. He didn't try to speak to her. Instead he pressed both hands tightly on her skin, willing her to be calm, willing her to blank out her mind, willing her to somehow receive if she could the computer's pulses. In this moment Blade wasn't thinking of science or of new knowledge. All that was in his mind as the pain exploded again was sharing with Arllona this last, miraculous chance for safety—if he could.

The pain mounted higher. Blade held his breath again, knowing that if he breathed now he would scorch his lungs. In another second his eyeballs would melt and run like jelly down his blistering, blackening cheeks. In another second—

The pain in his head leaped upward like the flames of the Mouth itself. Blackness swallowed him up, blackness and a deadly cold wind that howled around him from nowhere. In one moment he knew only searing heat, in the next he knew only freezing cold. He did not know what had happened to Arllona; he could feel nothing under his hands where she had been.

Then he could feel nothing at all.

Chapter Eleven

Katerina Shumilova's first sensation was a totally agonizing headache. She remembered how she had felt before losing consciousness in the chair far below the Tower of London. A giant hand had been crushing her skull. Now she felt as if someone had tried to put her skull back together again and had done a miserably poor job of it.

Even that disagreeable memory was reassuring. If she could remember something like that, it proved she was still alive, with a more or less functioning brain. She would have felt much better without the headache. She felt that her head would drop off her shoulders, or at least start falling apart, if she moved an inch or even opened her eyes. She didn't know if she was sinking into bottomless quicksand, or if a man-eating tiger was about to leap on her. She did know that nothing could be worse than what would happen to her if she tried to move. She lay still, and soon she drifted off to sleep.

The next time she awoke her head still hurt, but now it was more like the morning after a liter of bad vodka than the total agony she'd felt before. She could also sense other things, outside herself—wet grass under her and all around her, cool against her bare skin, a warm, scented wind blowing over her, grass rippling, leaves rustling, the drone of insects, the soft pad-pad-pad of feet—

Realization of what this meant exploded in her head

like a new stab of pain. What was she doing in a forest when she had been far below the Tower of London? This couldn't even be an English forest—it was much too warm for England in November. She was still naked—she could feel grass or warm air against every bit of bare skin. *What had happened to her?*

Fear fought with scientific curiosity for a moment. Then she opened her eyes. She gasped at the sudden blaze of light, as though someone had set off a flashbulb into her eyes, then buried her face in the grass again. The next time she opened her eyes, she did it slowly.

She continued to lie still until she thought she had the strength to get to her feet. Then she maneuvered elbows and knees into position, and lurched upward. Several small animals gave a startled *yeeeep!* and vanished in the long grass. Katerina staggered to her feet and stood upright. She realized that either she or the trees around her were swaying rather badly.

Her head was swimming, but it was her stomach that betrayed her. Sudden nausea welled up in her. She knelt down and was violently sick. She went on being sick, retching and heaving desperately, until there was absolutely nothing left in her stomach. She felt drained dry and her head was throbbing again, but otherwise she felt better than she had since arriving—wherever she was. She managed to get to her feet again and stagger away a few steps, to sit down in a patch of fresh grass with her back to a large tree.

After a while she still felt weak, but she could look around her and understand what she saw. She didn't like it.

She was sitting in a patch of long lush grass and trailing vines, with dense forest all around. Not just forest—tropical jungle. Some of the trees or the vines twining around them practically dripped brilliantly colored blossoms. A flock of strange birds with broad red wings and lean blue bodies flapped up from one tree as she watched. High above, clouds like puffed cotton ambled across a blue sky.

The damned British had certainly gone to a lot of trouble to dispose of her after the experiment! They had gone on drugging her, loaded her aboard a plane, then flown her down to South America or perhaps Africa—

somewhere a long way from London, and probably a long way from civilization. Well, she would just have to head back as fast as she could.

She wished that they'd given her some clothes, though. Modesty didn't concern her. What did concern her were insects, thorns, and night chills, in that order. Katerina muttered a few heartfelt curses at the British in general and at J and Lord Leighton in particular. Then she pulled herself to her feet and started forward, across the clearing and into the forest.

Deep under the trees there was so little light that practically nothing grew on the forest floor. If she hadn't had her field training in the endless forests of Siberia, she would have been lost within minutes. As it was, it wasn't until the ground started sloping downward that she could be sure of not going around in circles.

She promptly set out to follow the downslope. In any land water flows downhill, and water would sooner or later lead her to what passed for civilization around here. She would have to make up some very solid cover story to explain how she came to be here, stark naked and alone. She had learned to lie with a straight face, however. If she hadn't she would never have survived even one mission, let alone years of them.

Before she'd gone very far she was streaming with sweat in the hot airlessness of the forest. Her hair hung damp, limp, and tangled with bits of bark and leaves. Rough tree trunks and razor-edged leaves scraped and sliced her skin, and the scrapes and cuts stung as sweat poured down over them. Insects swarmed around her, forming a cloud in front of her eyes, whining maddeningly in her ears, biting and stinging. At first she tried to wave them off. Then she found that that took too much of the strength she was going to need just to stay on her feet.

Somehow she managed to keep going long enough. Toward the end her head was swimming, her eyes were dimmed with tears and fatigue and swollen half-shut with insect bites, her legs seemed to be made of lead, and her head started throbbing again. But the end of the forest did come. At last she stumbled out of the dimness onto the brush-grown bank of a river.

Katerina collapsed on the grass in the shade of a bush overgrown with pale red berries and stared out across the water. It flowed sluggishly past her, brownish-green, and at least a hundred meters from shore to shore. On the opposite bank rose more forest, a green mass as solid as the one behind her.

After a while she felt her strength returning. She walked over to the bank, bent down, and scooped water out of the river with her cupped hands. At this point she felt she would rather die from anything that might be in the water than die of thirst.

Drinking the water cleared her head still further. She took a firm grip on a projecting root and lowered herself into the river. The current was too gentle to break her grip, and the cool water flowing over her skin washed away sweat, fatigue, the stinging of her cuts and the smarting of insect bites.

While she was bathing, three of the red-winged birds flew down and began eating the berries off the bush. Katerina recalled another point of her survival training—anything the local birds and animals eat can probably be eaten by human beings too. She climbed out of the river and stretched luxuriantly to finish uncramping and unkinking her muscles. Then she walked to the bush and began picking berries.

The berries were hard and fleshy, but pleasantly sweet. She ate slowly at first, then faster, as nothing seemed to be going badly wrong inside. Even the first few mouthfuls of berries fought off the gnawing emptiness in her belly.

As she ate, she looked up and down the river. Down-river was nothing but forest and greenish-brown water flowing away into a seemingly endless distance. Upstream, the forest ended only a few miles away. Then the land rose, as green hills gave way to a solid wall of gray rock across the horizon. The direction of the sun told Katerina that she was looking north at the mountains.

In the center, the gray rocks leaped still higher, into an enormous cone-shaped mountain mass rising at least fifteen thousand feet above the forest. After a second look, Katerina realized that the cone shape was that of a volcano. A third look told her that the white plume from the broad summit was not wind-whipped snow, but steam. Apparently there was still life in the huge volcano.

That in turn made her suspect she was in South America. That continent had a good many live volcanoes, while as far as she remembered Africa had none. Absently she reached for another cluster of berries, while trying to guess which volcano this one might be.

Then a loud splash sounded in the water, fifty meters off to Katerina's right. She turned to look, and froze on the spot. *Something* large and scaly was climbing out of the river, water sluicing off a broad back set with twin rows of spines running from neck to tail. A red-eyed head with a two-foot parrot's beak rose, then the beak clamped down on a bush. The bush was ripped out by the roots. The creature heaved itself the rest of the way out of the water, stood for a moment on four splay-clawed feet, then lumbered off into the forest, the bush still clutched in its beak. From nose to tail it was at least ten meters long.

Katerina stayed frozen where she was long after even the sound of the beast's departure had died away. She was no longer afraid of the animal. What froze her now was a sense of facing the unknown, an unknown many times worse than anything she'd ever imagined.

There was no animal like that monster in South America. There was none in Africa. There was none any place on earth, and there hadn't been any for more than thirty million years. That thing was a creature of another world or another time, or both.

It seemed impossible and incredible. But could it possibly be so? Had the British mastered the secret of time travel? To dispose of her, had they hurled her back to the age of the dinosaurs? Perhaps she was alone in this forest, alone on this day millions of years before even Man's remotest ancestors would appear.

If she was that alone, she would be alone for the rest of her life. She did not cry, or faint, or even shiver at the thought. But for a long time, she sat completely frozen.

Chapter Twelve

Blade awoke with a headache that pounded and throbbed and seemed to shoot pulses of pain off to every part of his body. It was the worst headache he could ever remember feeling after a return to Home Dimension. He lay there, letting the headache shut out the rest of the world. He remembered Arllona and his desperate effort to snatch her away from the flames of the Mouth of the Gods in Kano. He also knew he ought to be up and asking about what had happened to her. For the moment he knew it would be pointless to try moving as much as his little finger, even to save himself.

Gradually the pain started fading from his limbs and body. Strange sensations replaced them. He did not feel the cool sheets of a hospital bed under him. Instead he felt damp moss, matted grass, dead leaves. He did not smell antiseptic hospital odors, but fresh growing flowers and rotting wood. He did not hear the whir of electronic diagnostic machines and the brisk click of nurses' heels on tile floors. He heard the sound of birds, the wind in tall trees, something large and alive crunching through bushes a good distance off. As the pain started to fade from his head, Blade opened his eyes and looked straight up.

Golden sunlight struck into his eyes, sunlight filtering down through a maze of leafy branches a hundred feet above him. All around were thick tree trunks, overgrown with preposterous tangles of flowering vines. The air was thick with odors, damp and warm.

Blade sat up, then felt both head and stomach settle down. His skin was reddened and smarted like a bad case of sunburn, but nothing worse. He stood up, brushed himself off, and looked around him again. The second look showed him nothing he hadn't seen the first time. This started him thinking.

Something hadn't gone the way Lord Leighton had planned it. He was *not* in London, or even in Britain. The forest around him looked like virgin jungle. If he was in Home Dimension, the computer had dropped him into the middle of Africa or perhaps South America.

That was a fair-sized "if." He could have also landed in some other part of the Dimension where Kano and the Raufi were now fighting it out. Dimensions were often complete worlds, as complex and varied as the Earth of Home Dimension.

He might also have gone sailing off into another Dimension entirely! That did not frighten Blade. He was about as incapable of being frightened as any sane man could be. But the idea of being bounced randomly about among different Dimensions was slightly unsettling.

In any case, it was hardly surprising that something had gone wrong. With the best of intentions, he had added a whole new factor to what was already a mass of unknowns by trying to help Arllona. What had that done to the computer's effect on him—or on both of them?

It was a waste of time thinking about it, he decided. He faced a mystery that even in Home Dimension would have been a monumental headache for Lord Leighton himself. It would just have to stay a mystery, for the time being.

The first thing to do here and now was find Arllona, if she was any place where she could be found. Blade didn't like the thought that he might have snatched her from the flames of the Mouth of the Gods to have her die miserably in this jungle. Looking for her, though, could end up like searching an entire field of haystacks for a needle that might not be in any of them.

Blade quickly scanned the patch of forest where he'd landed, carefully examining the ground and the trees. Within minutes he found a fresh depression in the moss, one that had the shape of a human body about the size of Arllona's. From the depression a trail of the prints of small bare feet led off into the forest. From a projecting stub of branch hung a tuft of long, dark brown hair—Arllona's, as far as Blade could tell.

Apparently Arllona had landed some distance from Blade, recovered consciousness first, then wandered off into the forest. Why hadn't she found him and waited for him? There could be various possible reasons for this, none of them particularly pleasant to think about.

Blade broke off a dead branch and traced the outline of Kano's flame emblem several inches deep in the moss and mold of the ground. If Arllona somehow came back here, she might recognize the sign and realize she should stay. Then Blade broke off another stick, one long enough and heavy enough to be a decent club, and strode off into the forest on the woman's trail.

Her trail was easy enough for an experienced outdoorsman like Blade to follow. For the first few hundred yards the trail wandered aimlessly back and forth, as though Arllona hadn't been quite sure which way to turn. Then it straightened out and ran straight for nearly a mile.

At the end of the mile, something had frightened Arllona into a dead run. The footprints showed the long, stumbling strides of someone running in desperation or blind panic. Several times Blade found more tufts of hair, caught on branches or vines and jerked out by the roots as Arllona had plunged onward. He moved on faster, trying to look and listen in all directions at once.

Another half a mile, and a tangle of fallen branches. Someone or something had plunged blindly into them, hard enough to snap the brittle or rotten wood in a dozen places, hard enough to cut and gouge themselves. The jagged ends of several branches showed the reddish-brown of drying blood. A closer look told Blade that the blood was almost fresh. He was less than half an hour behind Arllona now.

He quickly circled the tangle of branches and picked up the woman's trail again. She was still running, but her footprints showed an irregular stride, as though she was stumbling or staggering as she ran. Blade was tempted to break into a run himself, but he realized he had to look and listen for her even more carefully now.

He was also alert for other sights and sounds. Arllona was bleeding and panic-striken. Every forest had animals that followed the scent of blood or were drawn by signs of panic and fear.

Blade had barely finished this thought when he heard a faint moan from ahead. He stopped and listened. The sound came again. It seemed to be coming from a human throat, but there was nothing human about it.

It came a third time. Now Blade could be sure that it came from a particularly dark patch of close-grown trees. Blade headed that way, skirting several fallen branches that thrust long thorns out in all directions. Jagged stubs and more red-brown stains showed that Arllona had plunged straight on through.

Just inside the trees her flight had ended. She lay sprawled facedown at the foot of a tree, covered with sweat, bruises, and still bleeding cuts. Torn earth under her fingers and toes showed where she had kicked and clawed desperately after falling.

Blade bent down, checked her for broken bones, then gently turned her over. Her breathing came in broken gasps, and her eyes were closed. Blade shifted her so that her feet were higher than her head, then began to clear the dirst and weeds from her mouth.

As he worked, he heard her breathing become deeper and more regular. Then her eyes flickered open. They would not meet his, though. They wandered aimlessly about, then closed again. Her mouth opened, and the same low animal's moan he'd heard before came out.

Blade grimaced. By some unknown miracle, Arllona had made the transition with him, from the Mouth of the Gods in Kano to wherever they were now. But it looked very much as though her mind was gone. Was he alone in this unknown jungle with an insane woman?

The next three days were an ordeal Blade wouldn't have wished on his worst enemy. At one time or another he was in danger of death from just about everything except boredom.

Arllona's mind was indeed gone. That was clear after the first day. She whimpered, she drooled, her eyes refused to focus. She could walk, but to keep her with him Blade had to tie a length of vine around her waist and lead her like a dog. She would eat and drink only if he put the food and water in her mouth.

Then there was the deadly windless heat of the forest, the endless twilight, the hunger, the thirst, and the insects. Especially the insects. They swarmed around Blade and Arllona. Some bit, some stung, some crawled over

75

their scratches or into their eyes and noses and mouths, some just whined maddeningly in their ears. They tramped along in the middle of a whining, buzzing cloud. The insect bites spread across their skins until they both looked as if they had some repulsive rash and Arllona's eyes were swollen half-shut.

On the fourth day they came to a small stream, and the worst of the ordeal was over. The water was muddy and scummy, but they were too thirsty to care. Blade scooped several small fish out of the stream and gutted them with his bare hands. They ate the fish raw. He also scooped up mud from the bank and smeared it on the worst of the insect bites. They looked even worse as the mud slowly dried on their skins, but they itched and smarted less. Most important, the stream offered some sort of *direction*. Following it gave Blade real hope of getting out of the jungle.

Just before darkness fell that day, the jungle offered solid proof that this was not Home Dimension. In Home Dimension there was nothing like the forty-foot *thing* that came crashing and crunching through the trees along the stream. Its hide was scaled, its feet were clawed, its head sprouted a triangle of horns, its jaw opened wide enough to swallow Blade whole and displayed a double set of foot-long teeth. It growled, it hissed, it muttered to itself, it made the ground shake. Fortunately it did not notice Blade and Arllona as they ducked for cover.

If he had been alone, Blade would have climbed the nearest large tree. But there was Arllona, who had never climbed a tree in her life. Blade had to lead her to the nearest bush and crouch under it with her until the beast went snorting off into the twilight. She was too paralyzed with fear to move or speak until the forest was quiet again.

They slept under the bush that night. That wouldn't keep them from getting eaten if the creature came back and was feeling hungry. It would hopefully keep them from getting trampled on.

The night passed quietly. In the morning they awoke, drank again from the stream, and started off. The stream grew steadily wider during the next two days' march. By nightfall on the second day they could see a wide patch of sky overhead. Judging by the position of the sun, Blade thought that they seemed to be heading roughly northeast. Beyond the treetops, Blade caught a faint shadowy hint of mountains on the horizon.

Blade caught a two-foot fish that night, using a strand of vine for a line and insects for bait. Even raw, the fish was like a feast. In another day or two the stream would probably be wide and deep enough for him to try building a raft. Then they could float the rest of the way down to wherever this water might lead them. It might not lead them to civilization. It should lead them out of this damned jungle!

The next morning they walked for only an hour before the stream flowed into a full-sized river. It stretched nearly two hundred feet from bank to bank, muddy green and sluggish, running almost due north and south. Far to the north loomed a wall of gray, rocky mountains. In the center the wall reared up into a massive volcanic cone, its summit trailing a long white plume of steam.

Blade guided Arllona to a patch of soft grass, then stood on the bank, looking up at the mountain and at the blue sky above it. They weren't safe yet. Their journey might not even be half over. But certainly they weren't likely to face anything like the jungle they'd left behind them. Now they would have water and fish for the rest of their journey. Now he could start looking along the bank for logs to tie into a raft. Now he could—

The unmistakable sound of fast-moving human feet broke into Blade's thoughts. He whirled, eyes sweeping across the jungle behind him. The sound grew louder. He snatched up his club and started toward where he'd left Arllona.

Before he'd covered half the distance, he heard an explosion of crackling branches off to his left. He whirled again, in time to see four dark brown men dash out of the forest at a dead run. He could see that they all wore feather headdresses and carried long, heavy spears. Three wore brightly dyed loincloths, while the fourth was stark naked.

Blade knew that he was too far from cover to get out of sight before the men saw him. He would simply be speared from behind. He dropped into fighting stance and raised his club over his head with both hands, twisting his face into a ferocious glare. When they saw him, the four would see a formidable warrior, ready to fight to the death.

Blade might have been made of glass for all the attention the four men paid him. They spread out along the riverbank, looking toward the jungle and raising their spears.

Blade had just time to wonder why they were doing this when his question was answered. Something large was approaching through the jungle, something that was clearing its own path through the trees like a tank and making the ground shudder as it walked. Blade heard the crackle and crash of falling trees, the thud of massive feet, hungry growls and grumblings. The naked warrior shouted an order to the other three. They moved farther down the bank, but slowly and reluctantly, looking backward at their leader.

The leader turned enough to catch sight of Blade. His eyes widened, and Blade saw the muscles of his throwing arm tighten. The spear rose and the point swung toward Blade.

Then a tree crashed down, close enough to send twigs and leaves flying into the clearing. The growl turned into a deafening bellow. An immense scaled head reared up out of the forest, a triangle of massive horns jutting out ten feet. Toothed jaws opened, wide enough to bite a horse in half.

The naked warrior raised his spear higher, shook it at Blade, then shook his head and pointed with his free hand toward the beast. Blade got the message. The warrior would fight him, after he was through with the beast. It was his prey, and Blade should stand clear.

Chapter Thirteen

The beast was not two hundred feet long and fifty feet high. It just looked that way as it lumbered out of the forest, ploughing a path through full-grown trees like a man ploughing through high grass. Probably it was no more than half that long or high. But the ground shook with each step it took, and when it threw back its head and hissed the sound was like an exploding boiler.

The naked warrior with the spear looked as small as a mouse as he stood in the beast's path. The spear in his hand looked as puny and useless as a toothpick. He stood his ground, though, raised and brandished the spear, shouted and stamped, and bellowed curses and war cries at the beast. Blade watched, partly fascinated, partly amazed, and partly appalled.

He knew he should gather up Arllona and slip away along the riverbank. However the battle came out, they could be long gone by the time it was over. The survivors, if any, would be in no shape to chase them. That was the only sensible thing to do.

For once, Blade could not quite bring himself to be sensible. He had never seen such mad courage or courageous madness as this warrior was showing. He wanted to see how this fight came out, and he hoped he would see the warrior walk away the victor. There wasn't much chance of that, but if it happened he wanted to be there to see it.

The beast hissed and raised its head again. Blade saw that several spears already jutted from its head and neck. The warriors or their comrades had already struck home, enough to drive the beast and draw it after them, out of the jungle to the riverbank. The beast's jaws and teeth glistened with fresh blood. The fight hadn't been one-sided.

The world seemed to explode now, as the beast noticed the tiny figure trying to get its attention. Its head rose as high as a three-story building, arching up and out on a neck six feet thick and covered with scales a foot across. The head swayed back and forth, as the spearman continued his furious war dance. Then it swooped downward.

A second before the head and the man came together, Blade saw what the warrior was trying to do. He was trying to draw the creature into a furious lunge, then leap aside, going in under the horns with a thrust to one eye. With just a little more skill and speed he could have done it.

The warrior leaped a fraction of a second too late. One

of the horns smashed him across the chest, crushing ribs and left shoulder. He sprawled backward on the grass without making a sound or letting go of his spear. He still didn't make a sound as the jaws closed on him, the teeth meeting with a *clak* as they tore through his body in a dozen places. He didn't let go of the spear, either. A last convulsive jerk of his right arm drove it into the beast's nose, hard enough to pierce the scales. It jutted out at an angle as the beast's head rose, the warrior still clamped tightly in its bloody jaws.

The beast went on rising until its neck was fully extended. It went on rising until the front legs were clear of the ground. As it reared it swiveled on its massive hind legs. Blade saw thirty feet of armored tail swing like a club, heard bushes and trees crackling and crunching, heard Arllona scream. He realized suddenly that she was directly in the path of the swinging tail, and he hurled himself toward where he'd left her.

Like the dead warrior, he was a fraction of a second too late. As it swung toward the fear-paralyzed woman, the beast's tail rose into the air. Arllona stayed where she was. Blade saw with relief that the tail should pass clear over her. But as the scaled mass rose, it smashed into still another tree. Wood gave way with a terrible crackling and splintering. The tree tottered, then toppled over squarely on top of Arllona. She had time to scream once in helpless terror. She screamed again as the tree crashed down on her, a long and completely terrible scream, screaming out her life as the falling tree crushed her into the ground.

The beast's tail swept over Blade's head low enough to brush his hair. The falling tree crashed down close enough for a branch to whip painfully across his ankles. He stood alone, as the tail thudded to the earth behind him, staring at Arllona's arm sticking out from under the tree. Then there was silence, except for the hissing and crunching of the beast as it devoured the last remains of the man who had faced it alone.

There was no silence in Blade's mind. There was a rage so physical that he could hear it bubbling in his ears like boiling stew. His eyes swept down the scaly length of the beast, looking and remembering. He remembered that the hunter had been going for the eyes. So there was the vulnerable spot.

A spear in one eye—All the spears he could see were sticking in the creature's head and neck.

Very well, he would go get one of those. Blade's massive legs churned, and he plunged forward. He sprang onto the beast's tail like an Olympic high jumper. The tail offered him a clear path up on to the broad back. He remembered that dinosaurs were slow-witted and sluggish, unable to respond quickly to a fast-moving danger.

Blade moved fast. He dashed up the tail, onto a scaled back as broad as the roof of a small house. His rage made him inhumanly clear-sighted and precise in all his movements. At each step each foot landed exactly where he aimed it. He never slipped, never stumbled, never slowed down. He heard the three surviving warriors shout in astonishment as they saw him, but he paid no attention to them. All his attention was on the great head that was getting closer and closer.

He ran off the beast's back, past its front legs, and onto the neck. A single line of three-foot spines ran up that neck. Blade kept on until the neck narrowed too much to give him safe footing. A spear jutted out of the neck just below him. He knelt down, pulled the spear free with one hand, and grasped one of the spines with the other. He began pulling himself along with one hand while he held the spear ready to strike with the other.

By now the beast had realized that something unusual was happening. It snorted angrily and raised its head, peering in all directions except the right one. Blade kept moving.

The beast snorted again, hissed explosively, and stretched its neck upward, the head twisting and turning thirty feet above the ground. The movement was so slow that Blade easily kept both his grip and his spear.

Now he was too close for the beast to turn and see him or close its jaws on him even if it wanted to. For a moment the beast stood motionless, giving Blade steady footing. He released his grip on the last spine, took the spear in both hands, gathered his legs under him, and hurled himself through the air.

He landed sprawling on his stomach across the scaly

nose. From somewhere that seemed incredibly far away he heard more surprised shouts from the three warriors.

The beast's muzzle was finely scaled and as slippery as wet glass. For a moment Blade thought he was going to slide off and fall thirty feet. Then he dug his spearpoint into the scales and stopped his slide. From a yard away a yellow eye more than a foot across stared at Blade. The beast seemed to realize what was happening. It hissed louder than ever and started to rear higher. The sound half-deafened Blade. He ignored it and stood up, each foot wedged firmly in place at the base of a horn. Then he raised the spear over his head and with both arms drove it down into the eye.

If the beast's hiss had been loud before, now it sounded like the end of the world. Blade braced himself harder and leaned forward on the spear, driving it in deeper. Blood and foul-smelling yellow fluid gushed over him. The spear point struck bone. Blade put all his weight and all his enormous strength behind one final furious thrust. He felt bone crack, splinter, and give way, and the spearpoint rammed itself down into the beast's brain.

The beast reared up as if it was reaching up to bite at the sky itself. Its jaws opened and shut, the teeth clashing and crashing together with noises like an enormous threshing machine. The hiss came again, then turned into a scream. A convulsion twisted the beast from the tip of its tail to its head. The head snapped forward, then back. Blade felt his feet slipping, felt his hands torn loose from the spear with a jerk so violent that it seemed to yank every one of his fingers out by the roots. Then he was flying through the air.

He flew high, turning over and over in mid-air. He had time to see the beast starting to topple, and the other warriors standing as if they were rooted to the ground. Then he plunged downward. A branch caught him, sending a burning pain up and down one leg. Then he landed.

Blade was expecting to smash down on the ground. Instead he landed with a tremendous splash in the river. Pure reflex made him exhale desperately as he went under, to keep the water from entering his lungs and choking him.

He went down so far that his legs sank up to the knees in the sticky, slimy mud of the river bottom. For a hideous moment he kicked and thrashed furiously, struggling to break the suction of the mud. In another moment he knew his lungs would fill with water and the dark river would do what the dying monster on the bank hadn't been able to do.

Then the mud let him go. Blade's churning legs drove him upward into the daylight, into the air. His starved lungs took in an enormous gulp of air. Then he paddled to the bank and climbed out, water and mud and strands of weed dripping from him.

Now to find out what the three warriors thought of what he'd done. For all he knew he might have barged into a religious rite and now be doomed ten times over for sacrilege and blasphemy.

The dinosaur was dead, sprawled full-length along the river bank. In its fall its neck and tail had smashed down still more trees and hurled them about like matchsticks. It lay completely motionless, not even the tip of the great tail twitching.

Shouts sounded from the other side of the body and the three warriors appeared. They sprang over the outstretched neck and ran toward Blade, holding their spears level across their chests with both hands. Blade crossed his arms on his chest and stood where he was to meet them.

The three warriors ran up to Blade, thrust their spears into the ground, took off their feathered headdresses, and hung them on the ends of their spears. Then they threw themselves facedown on the ground in front of Blade, hands outstretched toward him.

If he'd done anything religious, it didn't seem like anything they were objecting to! It looked more like those warriors were worshipping him. Blade let them lie for what seemed like a dignified length of time, then spoke.

"Rise up. I would look on the faces of brave warriors."

One of the three warriors slowly rose to his knees. "You cannot mean that. We are as nothing compared to you, who have done what no Hunter of the Ganthi has ever dared do. We are barely worthy to wash the feet of your woman."

That reminded Blade of Arllona. He grimaced. "My woman has no more need of any aid, except that of men to bury her. The creature slew her, so I slew it." He motioned to all three men. "Rise, I said. The Hunters of the Ganthi need not be ashamed before any man of any people."

All three Ganthi warriors rose uncertainly to their feet, brushed themselves off, and retrieved their spears and headdresses. The first one to speak turned to the others.

"Brothers of the Hunt, we shall return at once to Thessu. The Eldest Brother of this Hunt is slain, honorably and bravely. So are the others of our band. We can do no more.

"We have also found a warrior not of the Ganthi who is worthy to be admitted among us. Perhaps he shall even be an Eldest Brother of the Hunters. Since the Ganthi lived in this land, such a warrior has come among us only five times. We shall bury our Eldest Brother and the woman of this warrior, then we shall return to Thessu."

The man turned to Blade. "I am Kordu. It is the law of the Ganthi that Strangers in our land must die, unless they prove worthy to live among us. You have proved that you are worthy. You have proved it ten times over!" For a moment awe at what he had seen Blade do overcame him and he was silent.

Blade nodded. "I thank you and your Hunters. It will be a pleasure to be among the Ganthi if all are such as you. Now let us go bury our dead."

Blade let the Ganthi bury the dead warrior first. This did not take very long, since there was hardly enough of the man left to bury. Then Blade led them over to where Arllona lay.

A last jerk of the dying beast's tail had hurled the fallen tree twenty feet away. Arllona lay exposed to view where the tree had smashed her into the ground. She was not a pretty sight, but Blade had seen more than his share of gruesomely mangled bodies. The face was almost intact. He knelt and rested one hand briefly on the pale forehead, then closed the staring eyes, stood up, and turned away.

He did not turn back until the three Ganthi had finished scraping the earth back over Arllona's body. He stood in silence for a moment, looking down at the grave. What could he say about Arllona, the girl who had lived a short and unhappy life in Kano and had met a wretched death far off in some other Dimension? That was about all the epitaph he or anyone else could give her.

"It is done," he said briefly to the three Ganthi. "Let us go."

Kordu nodded, picked up a spear drawn from the dead beast, and handed it to Blade. "By custom no one may bear a spear until he has received it at the Warriors' Feast. But I say you are worthy to bear that spear now."

"I thank you, Kordu," said Blade. He took the spear and fell in behind Kordu as the warrior led the way toward the jungle.

Chapter Fourteen

Katerina Shumilova left her camp by the river at dawn. She would have liked to stay longer. The camp had become as much of a home as any place in this world could be for her.

The British *had* discovered time-travel. They had sent her back into the past, into the age of the dinosaurs. She had seen and heard too much in the past week to doubt it any longer. Flying reptiles with twenty-foot wings, snakes forty feet long, a scaled horror stretching seventy feet from a horned and fanged head to a tail thicker than she was. There were other things that were only crashings in the jungle, shapes under the surface of the river, shadows and dreadful cries in the darkness. She was alone as no other human being had ever been alone. She would be alone as long as she lived.

Some people might have decided that there was no reason to move anywhere and have sat themselves down to die. Katerina was not one of them. She would go on fighting to survive as long as she was alive. Part of this was sheer toughness, part of it was her training. Part of it also was the memory of her father, Pavel Shumilov.

A fighter pilot in the Red Air Force, Captain Pavel Shumilov had been shot down behind German lines in 1943. Both legs broken in the crash, he had dragged himself along, through snow and wind and sub-zero cold, had dragged himself along for five days until he met a Russian patrol. After many painful months in the hospital, he had returned to combat. He had ended the war a Hero of the Soviet Union, an ace with more than thirty German planes to his credit.

So if Katerina did not give up, it was partly because she was the daughter of a man who hadn't given up either.

There were also practical reasons for moving on. There might be better food and water someplace else. There certainly should be some part of this land not completely overrun with dinosaurs. She had seen too many that could swallow her at a gulp, and she preferred to live without them as neighbors. Finally, scientific curiosity was still alive in her. Even though she knew she would die in this land, she wanted to die after learning as much about it as she could.

So that morning she put aside the last of her fear and headed south along the riverbank.

She was no longer naked or defenseless. She wore a hat and a robe, which she had sewn together from large, heavy leaves, using vegetable fiber for thread and fish bones for needles. Other leaves were tied around her legs with strips of bark, and still more strips of bark protected her feet. In one hand she carried a broken branch heavy enough to make a good club. All this made her feel like a human being, rather than an animal. The water and the fish from the river would keep her strong as she moved along the river. She was as well off as she could hope to be here and now, and before long she found herself whistling Russian folk tunes as she strode along.

The sun climbed higher. After walking for about three hours Katerina started looking for a place to rest. Then suddenly she wrinkled her nose and stopped. A puff of hot air blowing up the river from ahead brought her the unmistakable stink of something very large and badly decayed. She slipped behind the nearest tree and peered along the bank. She had seen the splintered bones of the victims of the carnivorous dinosaurs before. This could be another one, and the killer could still be around, feeding on its victim.

Katerina watched and listened carefully for a few minutes, saw nothing except large green birds flapping clumsily upward, as though they were gorged, and heard nothing except the normal rustle of leaves and drone of insects. The killer had fed and gone, leaving its victim to the scavengers.

As she moved forward, the smell grew rapidly stronger, until it was nearly overpowering. A few more steps brought her around a line of young trees and in sight of what lay dead beside the river.

It was one of the three-horned monsters, far larger than any she'd seen before, already bloating as well as stinking in the tropical heat. Several more scavenger birds flapped upward from a gaping red trough in the flesh of its back as they saw Katerina. Grim determination and scientific curiosity kept her stomach under control. This would almost certainly be her best chance to examine one of these monsters. She moved closer.

As she did, she realized there was something odd about the body. Except for where the birds had feasted, it was intact. Smashed and broken trees lay all around it, so clearly the beast had died violently. But whatever had struck it down hadn't fed on any part of the body Katerina could see. Had it been struck by lightning, or perhaps bitten by a snake?

Katerina stepped forward again, climbed up on the trunk of a fallen tree, then stopped so abruptly that she nearly lost her balance and sprawled forward off the log onto her face. Then she sprang backward, flattening herself on the ground behind the trunk.

She'd seen the head and neck clearly, and she'd seen half a dozen spears jutting out of the scaled skin or lying on the ground.

Katerina's fingers dug into the bark of the fallen tree as she fought the paralyzing astonishment and the fear sweeping through her. Somewhere in this jungle lived— some creatures, perhaps men, perhaps not—able to make and use spears. Not primitive spears, either—at least one of them had a heavy iron head a foot long. And that meant—

Katerina deliberately stopped thinking for a moment. She knew that if she tried to sort out all at once everything this might mean, she might panic. She could not do that. She would not do that. She would clear her mind and calm herself. She *would*.

Eventually she did. Then she began sorting out her thoughts. There were intelligent creatures, perhaps human beings, living in this world. Men and dinosaurs had never existed on Earth at the same time. The last dinosaurs had been dead many millions of years before Man's first and remotest ancestors had appeared.

Perhaps the spearmakers were not men. Perhaps they were another intelligent race that had existed on Earth in the time of the dinosaurs, one that had vanished without leaving any traces at all. Had they evolved on Earth along some lines that scientists hadn't yet even imagined? Or had they possibly come from somewhere other than Earth?

Katerina ran the arguments back and forth in her mind, looking at them as calmly and carefully as she could manage. She couldn't come up with any real answers. This might not even be Earth, for all she knew. The British might have discovered a method of transmission not only through time but through space as well. She might be—she shuddered at the thought—*light-years* from Earth. In that case, the spearmakers were certainly not human.

At this point she stopped arguing with herself. She realized that she was once again about to frighten herself into panic or paralysis. She didn't like any of the possibilities she faced, and she didn't mind admitting it.

All of the possibilities meant the same thing. She was not alone in this jungle. She would not have to play Robinson Crusoe to the end of her life, however long or short that might be. Sooner or later she would meet the spearmakers. She stood up and walked up to the body.

Close up, it was obvious what had killed the monster. Three feet of spearshaft jutted out of one eye socket. The spear had either been thrown with tremendous force and accuracy or else driven in from close at hand.

A few minutes' more exploring the area turned up two fresh graves, no more than a day or two old. Katerina was tempted to take a spear and dig up one of the bodies. That would answer the question of what sort of being the spearmakers were.

But the day was hot, the smell of the decaying carcass was about to make her sick, and something inside her balked at descrating a grave. Besides, the spearmakers might be rather touchy about their graves. Many primitive peoples were, she recalled.

Instead she took two of the spears. They had heavy wooden shafts and solid iron heads, but they were well made and well balanced. She swung them up on her shoulder and headed on down the river. It was nearly half an hour before the air around her no longer stank of a hundred feet of decaying dinosaur.

By now it was close to noon. Katerina crawled under some bushes, making sure to brush out her trail as well as she could. Under the bushes the air was stiflingly close. But there was shade, and with luck she would be hidden from anything—dinosaur or spearmaker—that might wander along. Enfolded in the darkness, she felt the morning's built-up tension slowly ease out of her. It was easy to fall asleep.

When she awoke, the sun was already well down toward the horizon. She grabbed her spears and scrambled out into the open. Then she picked out a convenient tree and began practicing throwing the spears.

Katerina was a natural athlete, with superb muscles and reflexes made even better by years of training. She found it easy to get used to the spears, not only for throwing but for thrusting and even for swinging like clubs. In half an hour she decided she knew everything about the spears she needed to, shouldered them again, and went over to the river to drink.

She was kneeling down, hands cupped to scoop up the water, when she heard a crackle of bushes behind her. She sprang up, snatching up a spear with each hand as she turned.

Ten men—ten entirely *human* men, as far as she could tell—were filing out of the bushes. They were brown skinned, lean, and naked except for feather headdresses, belts, and loincloths. Each carried two spears slung over his back and a club hanging from his belt. Each one turned to stare at Katerina as he emerged into the open. The stares did not look at all friendly.

Chapter Fifteen

Katerina felt one moment of an overwhelming sense of relief. Whenever and wherever she was, the spearmakers were apparently human. Or at least they weren't nine feet tall, three feet wide, and six feet long, with two heads, six arms, a tail, and bright blue skin covered with purple feathers.

The stares of the ten men were so hostile that the feeling of relief vanished after that one moment. Katerina wondered if she'd made a mistake in greeting them with her spears in her hands. Empty hands were an ancient gesture of peaceful intent. But it went against her training and instincts to disarm herself this close to an enemy.

Slowly and carefully she lowered both spears, until the points rested on the grass. That way they did not threaten the natives, but she could still easily raise and hurl them.

None of the ten men unslung a spear or raised a club. They stood silently like so many statues carved from dark brown wood, glowering at Katerina. She fought down an impulse to turn and run for cover. The nearest cover that would stop a spear was a good fifty meters away. She couldn't hope to get that far without at least being wounded. Alone in this jungle and hunted by men who knew it, she would have a slim chance at best. Wounded, she would have no chance at all.

Minutes passed. The sun was sinking down in the west, but it was still stiflingly hot. Only the faintest breeze blew in from the river. Katerina felt sweat trickling down her face and thighs. The faces of the men still showed hostility. Now they also began to show curiosity. They might be wondering at her pale skin, blond hair, and odd clothing. So far they'd shown no sign of realizing that they faced a woman. Her improvised robe of leaves was as shapeless as a tent. As long as it stayed in place she'd be able to conceal her sex.

Finally nine of the men formed themselves into two clusters, one on either side of the tenth man, who wore a blue loincloth and a blue headdress. Each man drew one of his spears and held it out in the same position Katerina was using, point forward and resting on the grass. Katerina acknowledged the gesture with a bow. Then she bent, took off her bark shoes, and tied her hat and hair in place with the bark strips.

She was going to have to fight. These people seemed to have the custom of giving even strangers a fair fight. That would help. Katerina was reasonably confident she could take any one of these warriors in a fair fight, perhaps two or three. Would custom also demand that she fight and overcome all ten in succession?

If that was the case, she would probably not live until sunset, and all her skill couldn't change that. Each fight would leave her weaker, facing a completely fresh opponent. Sooner or later the end would come.

She accepted this fact, hoped the end would come quickly, and put the matter out of her mind. There was no fear in her any more. She stared hard at the leader who would be her first opponent. He stared back, his face now completely expressionless. Then he raised his spear high over his head and twirled it.

"Hai, Stranger! Are you ready for the Rites of Meeting?"

Katerina's fingers suddenly lost all their strength and her spears thudded to the grass. A desperate effort at self-control kept her from doing anything else. She slowly shook her head, keeping her eyes on the leader as she tried to grapple with what had happened.

It *had* happened. She could not doubt that unless she wanted to believe she was going mad. She did not want to believe that. So what had happened was real, however impossible it might seem—except that if it was real, then it wasn't impossible, and—She desperately shut off that line of thinking and tried to tell herself what had happened in a few simple words.

The leader spoke in his own language, a series of growling guttural sounds. That was what her ears had heard. In her mind they registered as plain, simple Russian words, as clear and understandable as a headline in *Pravda*. She knew exactly what the leader had said, completely, clearly, and perfectly.

She might not be going mad. But certainly there was something in her mind that hadn't been there before. Something had happened to her brain when the British hurled her out of the Tower of London and out of the world she knew. Somehow, something—

Katerina realized that if she was not mad now, she might go mad if she spent much more time speculating on what had happened. She might also make herself an easy prey for one of the spearmen, which would be ridiculous. She would stop trying to comprehend the incomprehensible and live with it as best she could.

She raised her own spear and called out to the leader, "I am ready. I am of a people always ready to meet their enemies." The words formed themselves in her mind in Russian, but they came out of her mouth in the guttural growls of the spearmen. She was not surprised any more. In fact, she smiled at the thought of being able to insult her opponents in their own language.

The leader was surprised at being addressed in his own language. For a moment his face showed it, then smoothed over again. The arm holding the spear went back, then snapped forward. The spear gleamed as it hurtled toward Katerina.

The spear came fast. Katerina moved faster. She dropped on one knee, ducking her head but keeping her own spears pointing toward the enemy. The leader's spear whistled over her head and stuck quivering in a tree behind her. It was still quivering as Katerina moved in to the attack.

She didn't know what the rules might be for this sort of combat. She only knew that she had to win each fight as fast as possible, saving her strength and avoiding even the smallest wounds. That meant a quick, deadly attack, taking the initiative and keeping it. Otherwise she had no chance of even lasting very long, let alone surviving.

She dropped one spear to the grass, raised the other over her head with both hands, and dashed forward. The leader raised his second spear and moved forward to meet her. Katerina went straight in at the man, watched his spearpoint swing toward her, and stopped two feet beyond it. Her arms whipped her own spear up, over, and down in a blindingly swift arc, striking with the butt rather than the point. The butt crashed into the leader's forehead. His spear jerked, then wavered as he sagged forward on his knees. A moment later he was stretched out facedown on the grass. Katerina knelt and felt his wrist. He was unconscious but still alive. Good. She wanted badly to win and live, but she would be happier if she could do it without slaughtering these people right and left!

She stepped back from the leader and looked at the other nine men. "One of you has met me, and there he lies. What is your custom now?"

Another warrior stepped forward, brandishing both spears. "The Meeting continues, Stranger, until you or all of us can fight no more. It will be you, for we are still nine Ganthi and you are but one."

So it would be as she'd expected. "Do not tell me that you are so good. Come forward and prove it." If she could make them angry enough to stop thinking clearly, it might help. Otherwise each warrior could calmly watch what happened to his predecessors and learn from it. If they came out in a blind rage, on the other hand—

Another spear came at her, aimed low. Instead of ducking, she leaped sideways. Again she moved faster than the spear. This one struck the ground, bounced end over end, and vanished into the bushes. The warrior did not give her a chance to attack. Before his spear struck the ground he was coming in after it, seeming to move just as fast. His spearpoint danced in front of him as he closed, making little jabs and feints.

Katerina stood her ground, holding her spear across her body with both hands, letting the enemy's point drive in at her. At the last possible second she dropped to her knees, shifted her grip, and whirled her spear sideways. The sharp edge of the point slashed into the side of the warrior's knee as his own point darted over her head. It slashed through the leaves of her hat and they fell to either side. The warrior was too busy to notice. His gashed and weakened leg threw him off balance. Before he could recover, Katerina rose to her feet and smashed the shaft of her spear across the side of his head. The man's skull did not shatter, but his cheekbone and jaw did. His eyes went blank and he toppled sideways. Before he struck the ground Katerina was springing back, clearing off the last leaves of her ruined hat.

She didn't have time to check if her second victim was still alive. Another man was coming at her. He held on to both spears and stopped twenty feet away, holding one low and the other high. The man's comrades seemed to accept his refusal to close in. That wasn't good. If her opponents could play a waiting game, they could force her to use up time and strength she couldn't spare.

She decided to try a trick of her own. She deliberately turned her back on her opponent. Then with her body screening her movements, she bent down and came up with her second victim's spear in her hands. In one smooth movement she whirled and threw.

The man tried to leap aside, but he wasn't fast enough. The spear took him in the thigh. He did not cry out, but his face twisted with pain as he drew the spear free. Blood was pouring down his leg as he staggered away toward his comrades.

Three up, three down, no one dead yet, and not a mark on her. Katerina realized that she was doing better than she'd believed possible. She also realized this couldn't go on indefinitely. There was nothing except perhaps their taboos and rituals to keep the remaining seven men from a mass attack that would certainly bring her down. The scholars said primitive peoples would never go against their taboos. Did the scholars think the taboos would make all seven warriors tamely submit to being knocked down, one by one? These warriors were not fools. Sooner or later her death would become more important to them than their taboos.

The fourth warrior walked out with his second spear still slung over his back. One hand held a spear, the other held his club. He stopped a good thirty feet away, then raised his spear. He and Katerina threw at almost the same moment.

The warrior's spear flew wide. Katerina realized, too late, that it was supposed to. By then she'd already thrown her own. As it left her hand, the warrior threw himself down and rolled to one side. Katerina's spear missed as completely as his. Before she could throw another, the warrior bounced to his feet and came at her with his club. It whistled about his head as he came on, bellowing and screaming, seeming to fly across the grass at her.

Katerina twisted aside enough to keep the club from smashing down on her skull, not enough to miss with her own thrust. Her point drove into the man's body just above the bulge of his stomach. She felt the iron grate against the ribs, then slide through and into the man's vitals.

The swinging club did not miss entirely. It struck Katerina a glancing blow on the hip, jarring her painfully and ripping away the lower part of her robe. She suddenly felt air against bare skin. Surprise paralyzed her—only for a few seconds, but that was still too long.

In spite of the spear rammed deep into him, the warrior still lived, still fought, still struggled to close and kill. With a choking sound, he lurched forward. His club fell to the ground, but his hands rose, reached out, clutched blindly, and tore. Katerina heard bark thongs and leaves ripping apart, felt the man's hands against her skin, and jerked herself back and out of his reach.

As she jerked back, her shredded robe fell to the ground. She stood stark naked in a half crouch, hands still gripping her spear.

The dying warrior saw that she was a woman. His eyes flared open, he lurched forward again, and his hands clutched at her again. This time Katerina leaped back in time, letting go of her spear. The effort of that final lunge was too much for the warrior. He gasped, gave a great choking cough that sprayed blood all over Katerina, and fell forward. As he fell, the spear drove the rest of the way through his body and the bloody point burst out through his back.

As the warrior fell, his comrades at last saw Katerina clearly. Their expressions changed with horrible swiftness. One moment they were spectators to their comrade's death. The next moment they were staring in amazement at the formidable warrior who had suddenly turned into a naked woman. The moment after that raw lust dawned on their faces. All six dashed forward.

Katerina turned and ran for the trees. That was her

one chance now—get deep into the jungle and somehow outrun or evade the warriors chasing her. She was still strong, still not yet winded. She might have a chance.

But she misjudged her path, by just enough to be fatal. She plunged straight at the nearest gap in the trees, eyes fixed on it. She didn't see the spear sticking out of a tree on one side of the gap, the spear thrown by the fallen leader. She ran straight into it. The hard wood of the shaft slammed her across the ribs, making her gasp with the pain, driving the breath out of her, slowing her just long enough.

In the clearing behind her one of the warriors pulled a cluster of weighted cords from his belt, raised them in one hand, whirled them around his head. Then his arm straightened with a snap. The cords and weights whirled through the air, straight to their targets. Katerina felt the weights tightening the cords around her legs, bent to claw wildly at them, lost her balance, and fell on her side in the grass. The warriors gave a great shout, six voices sounding like one, and rushed up to her.

Katerina screamed then, all hope gone and raw fear bubbling up uncontrollably in her. She screamed and went on screaming, while her fingers still struggled to unbind her legs, a last reflex of the fighter she had been. The screams of a frightened woman and the struggles of the fighter both went on until one of the warriors stepped up and kicked her in the stomach. Then she was writhing silently on the ground, arching her body, trying not to choke as her stomach emptied itself. She stopped writhing only when the first of the warriors threw his loincloth aside and fell on her, with all his weight and lust and brutality.

Her last coherent thought was a wish that she'd killed or crippled one or two more of the warriors. That would shorten the nightmare. Then she gave into the nightmare of pain and pounding bodies, because she couldn't do anything else.

Chapter Sixteen

Katerina came slowly back to consciousness. It was a while before she was aware of anything except pain—pain in her head, pain in her stomach and back, pain in her groin and thighs, pain everywhere. The pains burned and stabbed and throbbed. She tried to sit up to vomit again, realized that her hands and feet were tied painfully tight, and turned her head to one side. She retched miserably for a long time, but her stomach was completely empty.

For a while it seemed that her mind was completely empty too. Then sounds and sights from the world around her gradually sorted themselves out. She was lying under a bush at the edge of the clearing. A look down at herself told her the pains were all real. From her breasts down to her thighs she was a mass of bruises, as though a dozen men had pounded on her with clubs.

Out in the clearing the leader was sitting on the grass, watching the six undefeated warriors digging in the ground with their spearpoints. The other three—the one Katerina had killed and the two she'd wounded—lay on their backs. All three were dead. Apparently these people killed those wounded who were too badly hurt to travel.

The leader now noticed that she was conscious. With the help of two warriors he staggered to his feet and walked slowly over to her. Katerina tensed. Was he going to take his turn with her now? She knew that she could not stand it, and that she would have to. She had been afraid and she was still afraid. She would not show it again, and *she would not die.* Or at least she would not die until she'd killed a few of these sons of bitches!

The leader stepped away from his two supporters and stood looking down at Katerina, swaying slightly on his feet. He seemed to be appraising her, like a meat-buyer appraising a collective farm's prize steer. When he finally spoke, she was able to listen almost calmly.

"Woman, you have been met by the Ganthi as are all Strangers who enter our lands. You have been defeated, as are all Strangers. The Ganthi are mighty warriors. If you were a man, you would now be dead, for our land is not for Strangers.

"But you are a woman. You are a woman who yet has the strength and skill of a warrior. This we have seen, we, the Brothers of the Hunt. We see only that which is true. So you are what you seem, and not what evil spirits may have put before us to make us afraid. I, Stul, an Elder Brother of the Hunt, say this." The other warriors bowed their heads at these words.

"You shall be taken to Thessu, and you shall live among the Ganthi as a woman taken in war. You will bear sons who will grow to be warriors and Hunters of the Ganthi, and daughters who will bear more sons. They will be strong, for you are a strong woman. This I say.

"I also say that you shall be first offered to Geddo, High Chief of the Ganthi. He is a man who needs many women, and takes them whenever he needs them. Those who please him may have great honor when they bear his sons. Think of this. I, Stul, say it."

Stul turned away. By now Katerina had prodded and pushed her sluggish wits into thinking up a strategy to improve her position here among the Ganthi. Or at least it would keep her alive a little longer. She pitched her voice to be firm but not too commanding.

"Stul, I would speak."

The Elder Brother stopped and turned, then stared down at her again, trying to read her expression. Katerina kept her face expressionless and waited. Finally Stul nodded. "You may speak."

"I am to be offered to your greatest warrior, is that not so?"

"It is so. Such is the High Chief of the Ganthi."

"Can I be given to him, unclean as I am? For you of the Hunters have indeed treated me as a woman, without any rites. You have made me unclean by the laws of my people."

"The laws of your people are not the laws of the Ganthi, woman."

"They are the laws *I* obey, Stul. I say this—you Hunters shall not make me unclean again. If you do I shall not be fit in my own eyes to be given to the High

Chief. I shall not let myself live to be brought before him. I was a warrior, I know how to bring death upon myself, and none of the Ganthi can stop me if I wish it. If I am made unclean again, I shall wish it."

It was a risky bluff, but not a hopeless one. Stul obviously hoped to give her as a gift to the High Chief of the Ganthi. She would be an unusual, even an exotic gift—a warrior woman—and Geddo would presumably be grateful. Stul would not want anything to happen to her between here and Thessu. If she threatened to kill herself if she was raped again, Stul might just possibly decide that he and his men should behave themselves. That would only give her a few extra days to recover her strength. But every little bit would help.

Stul stood in silence for quite a while, head tilted sideways and one hand stroking his chin. He was either thinking deeply or trying to give that impression. Finally he nodded.

"It is understood. You shall be permitted to become clean again according to your own laws. It shall be done before we reach Thessu. I, Stul, say this."

"How far is it to Thessu?"

"Seven days, not less."

"That will be as much time as I will need." She kept her voice level and her face straight. She wanted to smile or even laugh. Seven days to look around her and make plans without fear hanging over her. Seven days she could put to good use—if Stul kept his promise and controlled his Hunters.

Stul turned out to be a man who kept promises even to woman captives, as well as a leader whose Hunters obeyed him. The week-long trip to Thessu was not exactly a luxury cruise down the Volga for Katerina. But none of her captors touched her again during the whole trip. In fact, they carried her most of the way on an improvised litter. They gave her the best food and water they could find in the jungle, and even let her bathe regularly. She felt her strength and self-confidence returning bit by bit as the pain of her bruises faded.

Of course she had to continue to appear humbled and submissive every waking minute. That rankled. She also had to carry out some convincing "cleansing" ritual each day. She solved that problem easily. Every evening she sat down in lotus position and recited for half an hour passages from her training manuals or from the *Short History of the Communist Party of the Soviet Union*. She found that by concentrating hard she could still think and speak in Russian, which made her recitations even more mysterious. Stul and the other Hunters were appropriately impressed.

Katerina was walking almost normally by the time they reached Thessu, on the morning of the eighth day. Something unusual was obviously happening in the town. Several large fires sent smoke clouds up from behind the mud and thornbush walls. Scores of cloth banners floated from spears held by warriors standing on top of the walls. Warriors, workers, and slaves were dashing about like ants from an upset hill. Many of the workers were leading animals—large lizards or things that looked like one-horned goats—or carrying heavy baskets of fruits and vegetables toward the gates of Thessu.

"It seems that they prepare a Warriors' Feast," said Stul. He shaded his eyes against the glare of the sun and scanned the walls. "Yes, it must be that. But how is this so? The Feast for this year is not for another season yet. I must ask what is happening before we bring this gift before Geddo." He was obviously nervous, and the other Hunters caught that nervousness. They formed a tighter circle around Katerina and increased their pace.

Just outside the gate they met another warrior with the headdress of an Elder Brother of the Hunt, leading out a band of a dozen Hunters. Instead of spears they carried woven grass baskets and large cutting tools of hard black wood edged with stone chips.

Stul grinned as he saw the other party approach. "Ha, Kordu! Is it that you and your Hunters now must perform women's work? What have you done to so displease the High Chief?"

The Elder Brother called Kordu ignored Stul's taunt. "We go to do what must be done that this Feast will lack nothing. This is work for any man who is not too swollen with pride. Far worse to leave anything undone for this Feast."

"Then a Warriors' Feast *is* coming? How so?"

Kordu grinned. "It is a mighty moment for the Ganthi. Only five times before has a Stranger come into our land and proved worthy of living among us as a warrior. Now it has happened again. And *I* was first among the Ganthi to meet him."

Stul smiled thinly. "What did he do to prove his worthiness? Turn you over his knee and spank you?"

This time Kordu obviously was keeping a rein on his temper as he replied. "He sprang upon the tail of a three-horns and ran the full length of it with no weapon in his hands. Then he took a spear from its neck and killed it with a thrust in the eye. It was the largest three-horns ever seen by Hunters, and he is the bravest Stranger ever to come among the Ganthi." Then he noticed Katerina. "What have you there?"

"A gift for the High Chief," said Stul. "She is a woman who knows the arts of war. A warrior woman will be a mighty gift for Geddo."

Stul was obviously trying to boast of his prize. Just as obviously he was feeling angry and thoroughly frustrated. For a week he had been expecting that everyone in Thessu would stand around and gape in amazement at his prize, cheering wildly as he presented her to Geddo. Now he was home, and everybody was too busy preparing to celebrate the arrival of this mighty stranger to pay any attention to him. Katerina wanted to laugh out loud at Stul's predicament.

Meanwhile Kordu continued to look her over. "Has she said of what people she comes?" he asked.

Stul shook his head. "She has said nothing. She has spent much time on the journey cleansing herself in the manner of her people. But it is not a manner that I know of."

"That proves nothing, Stul. You are not noted for your wisdom or for your long memory of anything except insults." Kordu frowned. "I wonder if she is of the same people as the Stranger. He also is much larger than most of the Ganthi. Like this woman he is pale of skin, although his hair is dark. We know little of his customs as yet, but—"

Shouts and cheers suddenly exploded from behind the walls of Thessu. Kordu broke off, turned, then smiled.

101

"I think you shall see the Stranger for yourself in moments, Stul. Such cheers mean that he comes."

Stul tried to sneer. "Is he so mighty, or have we grown so weak, that we shout like children when he comes?"

Kordu shrugged. "Go and also slay a three-horns singlehanded, as this man has done. Then you will find out if we will cheer you as we cheer this—ah, here he is." Kordu pointed at the gate, where a tall man was striding out into the sunlight. Katerina's eyes followed the pointing finger. Then she stared, and went on staring, while the strength seemed to drain out of her so that she had to fight not to collapse on the ground.

The man walking out of the gate toward her was Richard Blade, the British secret agent from Lord Leighton's Project. He was thinner, dark with dirt and sunburn, bearded, and dressed as an Elder Brother of the Hunters of the Ganthi. But he was Richard Blade, alive and sane and healthy here among the Ganthi, in this time and this place. He was Richard Blade—or she, Katerina Shumilova, was finally going mad.

She was not going mad. She still would not go mad. She would live and fight. But she knew there was one thing she would not do now, because there was no sense in it.

She would not even try to guess where and when she was until she had talked to Blade. She did not know enough and she could not know enough about this world until then.

Of course, he was a British agent. On Earth he was an enemy, and there would be no sense in asking him what was going on, or expecting him to answer. But here—wherever "here" was—he was the only person who might know what was going on. She was someone who desperately needed help. A minute ago she would have been ashamed to admit that. Now it made no difference whether she admitted it or not. It was true.

Would Richard Blade see who she was and how badly she needed his help? If he saw, would he help?

Chapter Seventeen

Blade's self-control was formidable. It was part of his professional skills, and it never deserted him, no matter where and when he might be, or what he might be facing.

He still had to fight not to show stunned surprise and bewilderment when he recognized the captive woman with the band of Hunters. Blade had a photographic memory for faces and knew at once who she was. She was the blond computer technician from the Complex, the new one. She was stark naked, and now thin almost to gauntness. Her hair was as tangled as a briar patch and her skin showed dozens of fading bruises and healing scratches. In spite of all this she held herself straight and her blue eyes gazed about her curiously and alertly.

At least they were curious and alert until they fell on him. Then they widened until they showed white. The woman staggered as if she had been struck and for a moment Blade thought she was going to faint. The two Hunters holding her tightened their grip. That and some miracle of strength and self-control kept the woman on her feet.

Blade controlled his surprise and started thinking again. He was going to have to do something to take the initiative. If he just stood there much longer trying not to gape like an idiot, other people would notice, wonder, and do the first thing that came to their minds. Blade was sure that would not be good either for him or for the woman. He had to get her away from her captors and under his protection. Anything else could wait. Otherwise she faced a grim future here among the Ganthi.

In the long run he wanted much more than just getting the woman decent treatment. He *needed* to talk to her, and that would be impossible unless she was under his protection.

Here she was in Dimension X, alive, reasonably healthy, apparently perfectly sane and functional. How had she wound up being sent into Dimension X? How had she managed to arrive here safely and survive? Did her being here mean that the problem of finding another person able to travel into Dimension X had at long last been solved? That was an exciting question, enormously important for him, for the Project, for England.

Besides, this was the second time on this one trip something bizarre had happened. The first time had been winding up here among the dinosaurs and the Ganthi, along with poor Arllona. Now there was this. WHAT THE BLOODY HELL WAS HAPPENING BACK IN HOME DIMENSION?

Blade took a deep breath, realizing that he'd nearly shouted that last question out loud. He strode forward until he was face to face with the Elder Brother of the Hunters who had captured the woman.

"This woman is of my people. I claim her and say that she shall pass to me."

"Who are you, Stranger who dresses as a warrior of the Ganthi?" said the Elder Brother. His face and tone were cold. "By what right do you claim her?"

"My name is Blade. What I have done, you know. I *am* a warrior of the Ganthi because of it. I may choose a woman who pleases me and who is not claimed by another. This woman is of my people. I claim her."

The Elder Brother threw back his head and laughed. It was an unpleasant laugh, and his stinking breath made it even more unpleasant. "I am Stul, who has captured this woman. I—"

"Have you claimed her?"

"No, but—"

"Then it is my right to claim her." Blade stepped forward, one arm reaching out to the woman. He realized that he was being tactless and abrupt, perhaps too much so. But Elder Brother Stul seemed to be a man on whom tact would be wasted. He also seemed to be a man from whom the woman ought to be rescued as soon as possible.

Stul reacted faster than Blade had expected. As Blade put a hand on the woman's bare shoulder, Stul lunged forward. As he lunged he snatched his club from his belt and swung. Blade jerked his arm back just in time. The descending club grazed his knuckles. Then he pivoted, clenching both hands into fists as he did. One fist crashed into Stul's jaw. The other plunged into the man's stomach. Stul sat down in mid-air, then collapsed on the ground, spitting out blood and loose teeth and holding his stomach. For the first time since they'd met the woman took her eyes off Blade, and stared down at Stul. Blade thought he saw her smile faintly. He reached to take her by the hand.

"Behind you, Blade!" screamed Kordu. Blade whirled, ducking as he turned. A spear cut through the air where he had been and skittered along the hard ground. The Hunter who'd thrown it backed away at the expression on Blade's face.

A second Hunter was either braver or less intelligent. He stood his ground and raised both spears, one held ready to throw, the other to thrust. It was Blade's turn to back away, until he could reach out to Kordu.

"Your tool, my friend."

Kordu looked bewildered, but handed Blade the long, stone-edged wooden tool. Blade gripped it in his right hand, raised it, and charged at the other Hunter.

Blade was on the man in the time between one blink of an eye and the next. The tool whistled down. The Hunter's thrusting spear rose to block it. Iron point and iron-hard wood met with a clanging crash. Blade let the impact jar the tool out of his hand. He had never needed it for more than the feint.

The tool was still in the air when Blade shifted to his real attack. He swung to the left, clamping both hands on the shaft of the Hunter's other spear. He jerked hard on the spear, dropped into a crouch, and kicked hard upward with his right foot. The Hunter was pulled forward at precisely the right moment. Blade's heel smashed up into his jaw. Blade picked up the spear as the man's hands relaxed their grip, and he rose to his feet as the man sprawled facedown on the ground. The other Hunters of Stul's party took one good look at Blade, then dashed away toward the gate of the town.

Blade looked around. Apparently he'd made the right impression. Few of the onlookers seemed sullen or dubious. A good many warriors and most of the free workers and women were beating their hands on their thighs and stamping their feet. Among the Ganthi that was the equivalent of enthusiastic applause.

Blade now stepped up to the woman, took her by one hand, and put his other arm around her shoulders. Quietly, so that no one else could hear him clearly, he shifted into English.

"What is your name?"

The woman's lips quivered for a moment. "Ka—Catherine."

"How did you come here? Tell me quickly."

"I—they—" Relief at her rescue seemed to be making it impossible for her to speak clearly.

"All right, then. You can tell me later. But I *must* know. I am sure you can see—"

Someone coughed politely behind Blade. He turned to see Kordu standing there. The man looked as nervous as a fighting man of the Ganthi could let himself do in public.

"Blade, you must know that you have made trouble for yourself."

Blade grinned. "With Stul? No doubt. But I doubt if that man could ever be my friend. I have met many like him. I do not think he will be a very dangerous enemy, though. Nor do I think many will take his side, among the Ganthi."

Kordu laughed. "You see clearly, Blade. No, Stul is not a friend to many. He is a strong warrior, but he thinks he is three times stronger yet. Stul is not your problem, though. Your problem will be Geddo, the High Chief."

"How will that be?"

"Stul was going to present the woman you have claimed to Geddo. He hoped to gain much favor by this. He was right. Geddo likes strange, strong woman. He likes even more teaching them how to be weak. He liked teaching them so much that not all of them survive his lessons."

"I see that Geddo would hardly be a better friend than Stul. What will he do to me if he thinks I am an enemy?"

"He will fight you, Blade. To the death."

"Whose death?"

"Blade, I ask you—be wise. Geddo is a giant, larger

106

even than you. No man—no *two* men—have ever defeated him in a fight. You have shamed him, for you
have tried to take from him the great pleasure of
teaching this woman."

"Kordu, do not arrange for my burial rites until I am
actually dead. Otherwise—is there anything I must do or
say before the fight with Geddo?"

Kordu looked toward the gate of Thessu. "No. I think
he will be coming out here to kill you as soon as he
hears of what you have done."

"Good." Blade picked up a second spear and drove
both spears point-down in the ground. "I shall wait here
for him. If he is a giant, he will be easy to see coming a
long way off. Nor would I insult the High Chief of all
the Ganthi by making him run after me."

He gently pushed Catherine forward, toward Kordu.
"I ask that you protect my woman until the fight it over.
If Geddo wins, obey the laws of the Ganthi. If I win, I
shall claim her again, and there will be no more talk."

"It shall be as you wish," said Kordu. He put a surprisingly gentle arm around Catherine and led her
aside. Blade squatted down between his two spears, eyes
on the gate, and waited.

He had told Kordu one small lie. If by some chance
he wound up losing to Geddo, he would *not* let the laws
of the Ganthi take their course with Catherine. He
would use the last of his strength to give her a quick,
merciful death.

Blade waited quietly. As the minutes passed, the
crowd around him grew thicker, as word spread of what
was about to happen. His duel with Geddo might not be
formal, but it would certainly be well-attended.

A few minutes more, and Stul groaned, spat out a few
more loose teeth, and sat up. His face was a mask of
blazing rage as he stared at Blade.

"Geddo will be coming soon, Blade. Then I shall have
the pleasure of watching him kill you the way he kills
those who are his mortal enemies. They die very slowly,
Blade."

"You are more likely to see Geddo die, Stul. I do not
promise that will be a pleasure, though."

Stul managed to sneer. "You talk, and that is all.

Geddo may be angry enough to cut off your manhood and let you live to watch him teach your woman."

"Stul, you also talk. You talk too much and too loudly. Must I knock the rest of your teeth out of your mouth before you shut it?" He reached for one of his spears. Stul had a sudden attack of common sense and fell silent.

Time dragged The air became thick with heat, dust, insects, and the smells of the growing crowd. Someone got a bucket of water and poured it over Stul. Someone else got two buckets for Blade. He poured one over himself, drank part of the other and gave the rest to Catherine.

Catherine was just starting to drink when a bellow like an angry bull's sounded from inside the town walls. A thousand pairs of eyes swung toward the gate. Blade saw Kordu turn as pale as one of the Ganthi could, and he rose slowly to his feet. He reached out and picked up his two spears.

"That is Geddo?"

Kordu nodded and pulled Catherine away. They joined the crowd as it drew back from around Blade, until he was standing in the middle of a clear circle nearly a hundred feet across. Blade walked slowly back and forth across the circle, testing the footing at each step. Good. He would have solid, level ground under him, and plenty of room. Now all he needed was his opponent.

The bull's roar sounded again, closer this time. The warriors on the wall and at the gate raised their spears and bowed their heads. Then the crowd between Blade and the gate started breaking apart. Above the crowd Blade could see an enormous bald head, crowned by an even more enormous mass of feathers, moving toward him.

Geddo and the dozen warriors escorting him pushed their way through the crowd, into the open circle. The warriors spaced themselves around the circle, waving their spears to urge the crowd back even farther. Geddo stepped forward and glowered at Blade.

Not many men in any Dimension could glower down at Blade, but Geddo was easily one. Kordu had not exaggerated. The High Chief of the Ganthi was nearly seven feet tall and must have weighed close to three hundred pounds. Very little of that mass was fat. Geddo looked large enough and powerful enough to pick up two normal Ganthi warriors, one in each hand, and crack their heads together like a couple of dolls. If it came to a close-in grapple and those gorilla-sized arms closed around Blade, he was going to have trouble getting clear. He swung his spears off his shoulder and moved toward Geddo with one in each hand.

"Ho, Geddo, teacher of women!" he called. "Are you ready to learn as well as teach?"

"No one will learn from you," said Geddo. "No, that is not quite true. They will learn from you how I slay those who have insulted me and taken my women."

"They will not learn that if you throw at me nothing but insults," said Blade. "Come, Geddo. The sun is hot, and the people do not want to stand around all day to see you die."

Geddo's head jerked in acknowledgment. A rippling sound of anticipation—sighs, gasps, whispers, a few prayers—went through the crowd. Blade turned toward Catherine, raised both spears in salute until he was sure he'd caught her eye, then turned back to Geddo.

He turned just in time. Geddo was in too much of a hurry to care about ritual or custom. The High Chief charged straight in, both spears raised and held ready for a thrust with either hand.

Blade stood his ground. The crowd would promptly turn against him if he showed what he considered common sense and what they considered cowardice. That meant sacrificing whatever edge he might have in speed and footwork, but there was no helping it.

Geddo came on, looming like a charging elephant. One spear was now raised high overhead for a downward thrust, the other held low and close to his side. Blade judged his moment, then launched his own attack.

His own thrust was low, with his left-hand spear. His right arm shot up, the spear held crosswise, to block Geddo's attack and perhaps break his arm as it swung down. Geddo ignored Blade's counterattack. He drove home his own as though Blade was standing helplessly, waiting to be struck down.

Blade detected that mistake in almost the same moment Geddo made it. His right-hand spear whipped upward. The shaft cracked into Geddo's arm just above the elbow. Geddo's spearpoint flashed harmlessly past Blade's ear. Pain twisted the High Chief's face, but he still managed to block Blade's other attack with a quick shift of his other spear. The two spearheads crashed together, spraying sparks on to the ground. Blade disengaged and thrust quickly, one, two, three times with his right. Each time he thrust a little bit faster. Each time Geddo blocked him. Each time Blade came closer to getting his point home.

That was good news. He had the advantage in speed he desperately needed. He'd also taken something out of Geddo's right arm. Not surprising. That whip-crack of the spearshaft would have broken the arm of a smaller man, and the pain had affected even Geddo. Now to try to get in a similar stroke on Geddo's left arm, then to push the fight to a finish.

The whistle, swish, and clang of fast-moving spears went on without a break as the two opponents stood and fought. It was all speed and strength of arm and quickness of eye, with no place for thought or footwork or very much strategy. Blade could have done better with more freedom of movement, but he did well enough with what he had. Several times he broke through Geddo's defenses to draw blood, while he himself remained unmarked.

After a few more minutes Blade began to realize that he was gaining the edge. Geddo was still fast, still strong, still enormously dangerous. But his breath came now in clearly audible pants and gasps, and sweat was pouring off him. The High Chief lacked endurance, and Blade knew why.

Geddo hadn't had to fight this hard for this long in many years, not since he was a much younger warrior in prime condition. In all those years his enormous strength had let him strike down or cripple all his opponents in a few minutes. Facing Blade, who was no man's easy victim, was a different matter. Geddo still said nothing, but the wary, uncertain look in his eyes told Blade that the High Chief was becoming aware of the situation. In a few more minutes he would be desperate. That would be the most dangerous moment of the fight. Then Geddo would take any risk to strike down Blade while he still had enough strength and speed. Then the fight would explode in a flurry of blood and die away as one fighter collapsed, dead or dying.

Blade fought with extra care and extra alertness now, watching for Geddo to launch his all-out attack. It had to come soon. Geddo was definitely beginning to slow down.

In a few more minutes Geddo had slowed enough so that the warriors and even the workers and slaves in the crowd all around could notice it. Excitement rose from the crowd as they realized what they were seeing and what they might see. Blade, the Stranger, the warrior who had wandered into the land of the Ganthi, was getting the better of the High Chief Geddo, invincible for more years than some of the younger warriors had lived. Geddo was bloody, Geddo was pouring out rivers of sweat, Geddo was beginning to pant for breath. In a few minutes Geddo would be down on the ground, his life flowing out of him. Then Blade would rise, and when he did, he would be the new High Chief of the Ganthi.

Blade hoped that he was breaking no vital taboo among the Ganthi. If he was, he had the choice between dying at Geddo's hands and being lynched by the crowd for killing the High Chief. Neither appealed to him, and both would leave Catherine helpless. He threw her a brief glance. Her face was set and pale, and sweat made trails in the dust on her skin.

The duel went on. Blade began pushing his attacks home faster and faster, taking more chances in order to do more damage. The more wounds the High Chief took, the slower he would be.

Once Blade took too big a chance. One of Geddo's spears pinked him lightly in the left shoulder as he pulled back. The crowd murmured at the first sight of blood on the Stranger. But that was the only time Geddo drew blood. Blade drew blood four more times. The High Chief was beginning to look like a statue of red mud, as the blood and the dust on his skin mixed, caked, and dried. Blade had to admit that the man had courage, and an enormous ability to take punishment.

But no man could go on much longer with as many wounds as Geddo had taken.

The two fighters were no longer standing still as they exchanged thrusts and slashes. Now they were slowly shifting position, one step at a time, circling around each other like a pair of fighting cocks. Blade threw a quick glance upward at the sun. They were slowly shifting toward a position where the sun would be shining in his eyes. That would be Geddo's best chance to launch his attack. Blade stepped up the pressure, determined to weaken Geddo still more. In the next three minutes, he drew blood three more times and took a slash across his left cheek. He could taste the oozing blood in the corner of his mouth. Geddo looked totally hideous, and he was beginning to stagger. Insects droned around his head, drawn by the scent of the blood. Blade looked at the sun again. In another minute—

Pain seared through the calf of his right leg. He bit back a yell of sheer agony and looked down. A hard-thrown spear had gone clear through the flesh of the calf. The bloody head stood out on one side, the shaft on the other. Shouts, yells, and gasps of surprise and confusion rose from the crowd. Geddo stared over Blade's shoulder. Blade turned and looked in the same direction.

Stul was trying to back out of sight into the crowd, his face drawn and pale. He had only one spear. Blade bent down, gritted his teeth, snapped the shaft of the spear, then drew it out. He had to bite back another yell of pain as he did, and the blood flowed freely as the spear came out. He was able to control the bleeding with a rough bandage torn from his loincloth. But he could no longer move fast on his right leg. In fact, he had to grit his teeth to stand at all.

Meanwhile Geddo glowered around at the crowd, his bloody, filthy face set in a terrible mask. Blade saw that no one would meet the High Chief's eyes. The message was plain. What Stul had done was contrary to all law and custom. But it had also given Geddo back the advantage in the fight. The High Chief would win this fight, slay Blade, and then be free to deal with anyone who might protest against what Stul had done. No one would lift a hand to punish Stul or help Blade. For

Blade, that meant the end—a quick and bloody end. For Catherine—

Blade looked toward the woman. She had gone a bleached white under her dirt and sunburn. He'd promised himself that she would not have to endure slavery to Geddo. He would keep that promise. Blade estimated the distance to the woman, knew that he could throw accurately that far, and was fairly sure he could give her a quick death with a spear to the heart. That would leave him with only one spear and nothing to do but launch his own last-ditch attack. He might still take Geddo with him.

The High Chief was raising his spears again and looking arrogantly toward the limping, slow-footed Stranger who would now be his latest easy victim. All Geddo's pride and self-confidence had returned. If the man would just go on striking that pose, showing off rather than keeping his mind on business—Blade raised a spear, aimed at a point just below Catherine's left breast, and got ready to throw. Another second—

As Blade's arm snapped forward, the ground under his feet heaved upward and sideways in one sharp motion. His wounded leg gave under him and he sat down abruptly. The spear sailed off wildly. He never saw where it went or what it hit. A sudden silence fell on the crowd.

Then the earth heaved again. The silence dissolved in a pandemonium of screams and yells. A thousand people or more were all crying out at once, cursing, praying to gods and ancestors, shouting out in fear and anger.

The earth heaved a third time. Blade staggered to his feet in time to see clouds of dust rise from inside Thessu as buildings collapsed. Part of the mud-brick wall went down in a whirlwind of brown dust, carrying a dozen banner-bearing warriors with it. Distant screams of pain joined the rest of the uproar.

Geddo stood in the center of the circle, staring wildly about him with a mad look in his eyes. He seemed stunned and numb. The earthquake had struck at the moment when he was tasting victory. Now he seemed unable to imagine what to do next.

Blade had no such problem. His wits had never

worked as fast as they did in the next few seconds, as he realized that the earthquake had given him a sudden, unexpected chance at victory.

He took a deep breath and let out a terrible wordless roar, louder than Geddo's, trying to beat down and drown out the noise of the panic-stricken crowd. Scores of heads turned toward him. He raised his spear and pointed first at the earth and then at the sky.

"The gods have spoken!" he thundered. "Stul's treachery has called down their wrath. The earth moves because of it. It will move again and again until Thessu lies in ruins if we do not turn away the wrath of the gods. Find Stul! Find Stul and slay him for his treachery! Offer his blood to the gods, offer his flesh and his bones. Turn their wrath away and save your city, save your land!" He was tempted to go on and ask them to slay the High Chief himself, but that would have been asking too much.

Blade's words struck home in the crowd. The sounds of panic began to fade, the sounds of anger began to swell. Spears and cries both rose.

"Slay Stul!"

"Cut his throat!"

"Take his manhood!"

"KILL!"

The crowd churned and heaved as people looked about them for their victim. Geddo continued to stare wildly about him. Blade raised his spear and sighted on the High Chief's blood-smeared chest. A single well-aimed spear, and—

Geddo exploded out of his daze and charged at Blade, both spears flailing the air. His eyes seemed blind with blood, dirt, sweat, and sheer rage. He still came straight at Blade, his feet leaving bloody prints on the ground.

Blade stood his ground again. He doubted if he could move fast enough to get clear in any case, with his wounded leg. He also knew that he could still turn the crowd back to Geddo's side by showing anything they would call cowardice. As Geddo charged in, Blade raised his spear in both hands and thrust forward with all his strength and all his weight behind the thrust.

Geddo did not stop or slow his mad-bull's charge at Blade. Instead he ran himself straight onto the out-thrust spear. The point tore through his chest and burst out his back. He screamed and kept on coming, his three hundred pounds driving him right up the spearshaft at Blade.

Blade held on to his spear as Geddo loomed monstrously over him. He heard the blood gurgle in the High Chief's throat and felt one of Geddo's spearpoints slash his right ear. Geddo choked and coughed again, drenching Blade in blood. Then he fell. Blade had no time to jump clear before the High Chief's three hundred pounds of dead weight hammered him to the ground.

Blade's head struck the ground so hard that for a moment the world spun crazily about him in a gray fog. He lay still for another moment, until his head started clearing and he could distinguish the roaring in his ears from the roaring of the crowd. Faintly, in the middle of the roaring, he heard someone scream, screaming three times in prolonged and terrible agony.

Then warriors and Hunters, with Kordu in the lead, were running out from the crowd, grabbing Geddo's body by the ankles and unceremoniously dragging it off Blade. Others bent over Blade and helped him to his feet. He lurched and staggered, but he managed to stand.

Another warrior ran out of the crowd, carrying something bloody in one hand. He threw it at Blade's feet. Blade saw it was Stul's severed head. Somehow he managed to thank the man, although it hurt him to speak. His throat felt as if it were filled with red-hot pebbles.

Then Catherine broke away from the warriors guarding her and ran toward Blade. Blade held out both arms to her and she ran straight up to him, flowing up against his chest. He felt her shivering and trembling, heard her incoherent murmurs in his ear, and held her tightly. Gradually he felt her grow calm and quiet.

Kordu stepped up to Blade and knelt as he had by the river after Blade had killed the giant three-horns.

"Blade, what is your will?"

"My will?" The words came out in a croak the first time. Then the thought burst in Blade's mind.

By his victory, for better or worse, he was now the High Chief of all the Ganthi.

Chapter Eighteen

The first thing the new High Chief of the Ganthi nearly did was fall flat on his face in front of more than a thousand of his new subjects. Blade was hot, horribly thirsty, and dizzy from pain and loss of blood.

Catherine chose that moment to faint in his arms, from sheer relief. He lowered her gently to the ground. Then for a while he was much too busy seeing that she was properly treated to worry about his own wounds.

He was also much too busy listening to what she babbled as she tossed and turned on her sleeping mat in the grip of fever and nightmares. He listened very carefully, and he did not like what he heard.

She babbled in Russian, to start with. Blade knew the language well enough to understand most of what she said. She was disoriented, and she thought she was in a hospital deep inside Russia, being cared for after returning from a mission in the West! Then she cried out and clutched at her head and stomach, moaning something about Lord Leighton, J, and a terrible gray monster of a computer.

She moaned and murmured and babbled a good deal more, and by the time she fell into a quiet, healthy sleep Blade knew most of what he had to know about Katerina, who she was, and how she had been sent into Dimension X.

Katerina was a Russian undercover agent. She had successfully penetrated the Project by getting her job as a computer technician. That in itself was going to mean a monumental uproar in Project Security. Probably the uproar was already underway, if Lord Leighton and J were moving as fast as they usually did when the Dimension X secret seemed to be in danger.

Somehow she had been detected and caught. Blade could easily see the logic of what had happened next. The best way of keeping the secret of the Project was for Katerina to quietly disappear. The best way to do that was to send her off to Dimension X. Whatever happened to her, she would never come back to Home Dimension with what she'd learned.

So far so good. But none of this explained how in the name of Whoever ruled Dimension X Katerina had managed to arrive here, alive, sane, and entirely functional! How had it happened? How had half a dozen picked Englishmen died or gone mad on trips to Dimension X, while Katerina hadn't? How had years of searching for someone else who could survive the trip been totally unsuccessful, if Katerina had done it so easily? *What had gone wrong?*

Blade realized that this trip into Dimension X was sprouting unanswerable questions like an untended garden sprouting weeds. Certainly they were unanswerable by anyone except Lord Leighton and his team of scientists, far away in Home Dimension. There wasn't too much Blade could do beyond observing what happened and staying alive to return to Home Dimension and report on it. It was maddening to have to play such a passive role, but unfortunately he didn't have much choice.

One thing he *could* do on the spot was do his best to get from Katerina the story of who she was, what she had done, and how she had managed to survive her trip. That raised a knotty question. Should he frankly tell her that he knew who she was, and that she shouldn't waste time with cover stories? Would he learn more, or less, if he did that? Would he be in more or less danger?

He turned the question over and over in his mind for several hours, and decided in favor of telling the truth, as far as he would tell Katerina anything. If she was as good an agent as she probably was, he had to assume that she knew who he was, and that she would be on the alert in any case. She would not really *expect* him to believe her cover story, which would certainly be lame and full of holes. There was no really convincing way for her to explain how she had gotten here! She would also be less likely to try extracting information from him, if he let her know that he was aware and alert. She would know then that probing him would be a waste of time.

Of course, there was the danger of setting up a total stand-off, in which neither could hope to learn very much about the other. As long as they were both in this

117

situation, however, there wouldn't be *too* much danger to the Dimension X secret. Blade knew he had to start by protecting that as best he could and letting anything else come second.

There were other methods for extracting information from Katerina without giving any himself. Blade had used those methods before, even on women. He never enjoyed using them on anyone, but he never hesitated when the need arose.

But here in Dimension X, it was hardly safe to proceed to drastic methods. He and Katerina were alone here among the Ganthi, and for the moment they would do better as temporary allies, guarding each other's backs. Threatening Katerina would certainly make her an open enemy, determined to destroy him at any reasonable risk to herself. She would be a formidable enemy, Blade knew. The Russians chose their top agents well and trained them better.

Even if Katerina did not kill him, an open fight between them would leave the Ganthi confused and wondering what was going on. The Ganthi might well decide to end their new High Chief's life. Blade could not afford to risk his own life that way in order to extract Katerina's secrets. Anything he might learn would be wasted if it died with him.

There were also two more considerations. First, Katerina might very well not make it back to Home Dimension, even with his help. She'd made the trip one way, but that didn't guarantee she could make it both ways. If she didn't return to Home Dimension alive and sane, it didn't matter how much she learned.

Second, she *was* somebody from Home Dimension, even if she was from the opposition. Without some good reason, Blade could not bring himself to simply kill, torture, or even deceive somebody able to survive the trip, somebody who was, by virtue of that quality alone, set apart from the rest of the human race, who was in a way his equal and his comrade. It would be like wantonly destroying a great work of art, to "terminate" or even endanger Katerina unless he had to.

It took Blade several hours of complicated analysis to reach his conclusions, and he was more relieved after reaching them than he had been after some major battles he'd fought. He sincerely hoped that Russian agents weren't going to start popping out of the woodwork on *every* trip into Dimension X!

It was early evening before Katerina fell soundly asleep and Blade felt he could leave her to have his own wounds cared for. He was careful to wash all of the wounds thoroughly in hot, herb-scented water, and he insisted that the bandages be thoroughly boiled as well. Then he ate a light dinner and returned to the hut where Katerina lay asleep. He sat by her bed as evening turned to night, as drinking and feasting in celebration of the new High Chief began outside in the streets of Thessu.

He was sitting there when she awoke.

Katerina awoke to find that darkness had come down on the town. She felt weak and tired, but clearheaded again. Then she saw the massive form of Richard Blade looming over her in the dim room. She gave a small gasp of surprise, before she realized that he was sitting calmly on the floor by her low bed, looking down at her. His cheek, leg, and ear were freshly bandaged.

He reached over and took her by one hand as he saw she was awake. "Welcome back, Catherine. You had me worried there for a while."

She laughed. "*I* had *you* worried? What do you think I was doing when you were out there fighting with Geddo? Doing trigonometric equations in my head?"

He laughed also. "No, I don't imagine you were. But it's still good to have you with us again."

"Us?"

"With me and the Ganthi. I am High Chief now, by defeating Geddo in fair combat. At least *he* had a fair chance."

Katerina nodded. "Is Stul dead?"

"Yes. They laid his head before me, just before you fainted. We don't need to worry about him any more. In fact I'm not sure that we need to worry about anything, at least not for tonight."

Katerina heard a particular note in Blade's voice as he said those last words. They made her more aware than before that she was naked under a quilt of woven rushes, and that he was naked except for a loincloth and his bandages. His huge body was perfectly conditioned, and it radiated a quality of power and competence she'd never encountered before. She could not keep her eyes from roaming over that body from head to foot. Nor could she limit her appraisal to the professional sizing-up of a possible enemy. A faint bell-like note of erotic interest was ringing deep in the back of her mind as she looked. There was the sheer physical appeal of Blade, there was the overpowering sense of relief at being for the moment out of danger, and there were other things she couldn't put a name to. She could not help imagining those enormous, powerful arms around her and that wide chest pressed against—

Without a word, Blade bent over, pulled the quilt back, and lay down beside her on the bed. For a moment he lay still, moving nothing but one finger that traced a gentle line along her cheekbone, down her throat, and over the firm curve of her left breast. She shivered and felt the nipple spring erect as the finger passed over it. He saw it and bent over it, his lips warm on her skin. Katerina felt another sort of warmth inside her, a tingling warmth, as though little jolts of electricity were flowing through her.

She hadn't expected this to happen, not with Blade, not after the rape by the Hunters in the forest. She wasn't terribly surprised either, and as the warmth spread slowly through her body, she knew she wouldn't stop. She couldn't even if she wanted to, and she didn't want to. All she wanted now was for Blade to sense what she was feeling and what she wanted, to take her in his arms, to do everything that she knew he could and would do.

For a moment longer Blade's lips and fingers continued their gentle movements up and down her body. Katerina felt the tingle become a continuous pulsing warmth, gasped, whimpered as desire rose in her, bit her lip to keep from crying out at the delicious agony. She tried to hold herself still, but she found her body arching upward toward Blade, her arms reaching out for him, her lips moving as passion drew wordless sounds out of her.

Blade kissed her full on the lips, and she let her mouth fall open and her tongue creep out to play with his as it seemed to search the inside of her mouth. Then he gave a faint groan of pain as he lifted himself above her on his massive arms. She had a moment of fear as she remembered how it had been the last time a man entered her, a fear that Blade seemed to sense. Effortlessly he held himself above her with one arm, while he stroked her cheek with the other hand. Then with a sudden graceful movement, he bent down and gently bit the lobe of one ear. In a moment the fear vanished. Katerina laughed out loud. She was still laughing as she felt Blade sinking down onto her and into her, and he was still stroking her cheek and murmuring gentle noises.

Blade was huge. In the first moment his massiveness was both exhilarating and frightening. Then the fear vanished and the exhilaration rose as she felt that wonderful massiveness beginning to move within her.

Blade rose and fell in a superbly controlled rhythm, sometimes withdrawing almost completely, tantalizing and tormenting her. In those moments she arched herself upward and clawed at his back and shoulders, desperate to bring him back down and into herself again. As other times he plunged deep into her until she wondered that she could hold him. Then she would lock her arms and legs about him, trying to hold him there.

All the while the warmth within her was growing. The little pulses and shocks came more and more often. She gasped, she moaned deep in her throat, she cried out little words in Russian and English, she made more wordless sounds, she felt tears starting from her eyes. She knew that her control was slipping, knew that in another moment she would be a writhing, howling animal.

Her control vanished. She did not know where she was, who she was, what she was doing, what was happening to her. She knew vaguely that the solid body above her and against her was twisting and writhing as wildly as hers was, that the massive solidness within her was jerking and spurting warmly into her. It was a very long time before she knew anything else.

By the time she did, Blade had rolled off her and was lying on the mat beside her, cradling her in his arms. Even then she had only vague impressions of his warmth, the darkness around them, the noises of the feasting and celebrating that floated in through the door of the hut.

She did know that before too long desire rose in both of them again. This time she spared him effort and strain on his wounds. This time she caressed every part of his body with her hands and her lips, straddled him, took him into herself, once again reduced both of them to animals. When she finally lay down on the mat, it was just in time for both of them to fade away into a dreamless sleep.

They slept so deeply, in fact, that they slept right through another earthquake that came in the night.

Chapter Nineteen

The third earthquake frightened everyone in Thessu. The new High Chief had promised that the wrath of the gods would turn aside if they killed Stul. Now Stul was dead and so was Geddo. Yet the trembling of the earth continued? People were bustling about nervously the next morning when Blade and Katerina awoke. Although he was greeted with deference, Blade caught some looks he didn't like at all.

Fortunately, the third earthquake was the last one. So the uncertain or suspicious looks at the new High Chief soon faded away. None of the quakes had done really disastrous damage, in any case. Thessu's houses and huts were built of logs, with light thatched roofs. They fell easily, but they hurt few people when they fell, and they could be rebuilt almost as easily. Most of the damage from the quakes was to everybody's peace of mind, and that faded away within a few days.

Blade soon found that being High Chief of the Ganthi was a comparatively easy job. He had to lead them in war. But there hadn't been a war in several years. He had to preside over the Feasts for the Warriors and Hunters. But there wasn't one of those scheduled for another three months. He had to accept any challenges that any lesser warrior or Hunter might issue. But after watching Blade fight Geddo and slay him, no one seemed at all interested in challenging the new High Chief.

It was also the custom for the High Chief to acquire and maintain a large harem of the loveliest women he could find among the Ganthi. Geddo had kept that custom very well, as Blade discovered. Most of the women in the harem he inherited were indeed beautiful. Too many of them also showed the marks of Geddo's "teaching"—scars, whip-welts, pulled teeth, missing toes, and even missing eyes. Even if Blade hadn't had Katerina, he would not have enjoyed living among these reminders of his predecessor's cruelty.

"You cannot set them all free, Blade," said Kordu. "Then they would think you do not desire them. That would be to lay a great shame upon them. Their families would become your enemies." He lowered his voice and added, "There are already enough who think evil things may come to the Ganthi from making a wandering Stranger the High Chief."

"The Ganthi have obeyed their laws in making me High Chief," said Blade. "It is always wise to do that. I shall do the same. I shall not set any of the women aside. Neither shall I go to them for one year. I have taken Katerina of my own people as my first woman. By the laws of my own people, a man may not take other women for one year after he has taken his first."

"Also, I think the woman Katerina would have things to say to you if you did not obey that law," said Kordu, with a grin. "Am I right?"

"You are right, my friend," said Blade. "Katerina and the women of my people are not as the women of the Ganthi. Neither gods nor men can make them so. I hope none among the Ganthi think otherwise."

"I have heard none such," said Kordu. "But I think I would do well to keep listening. I call you friend as well as Chief, Blade. Both as friend and Chief you may need an extra pair of ears in places where you may find it hard to go yourself."

"I thank you, Kordu. You are a wise man as well as a friend."

As hard as Kordu listened, he heard nothing for a long time. Blade settled into a quiet routine that would have swiftly become murderously boring, if it hadn't been for Katherina.

She was neither surprised nor frightened when he revealed that he knew who she was. In fact, a frank discussion revealed that she had come to many of the same conclusions he had about their relationship while in Dimension X. She was a highly intelligent and sensible woman, politically orthodox (the KGB wouldn't use any other kind), but not so fanatical that she insisted on playing spy games when they would be suicidally risky.

After settling that point, Blade was able to find excitement and pleasure in his relationship with Katerina. There was raw, hot joy in making love to her, taking his pleasure from her superb body and giving pleasure back just as generously. Their sex had begun almost by accident, but it had begun well. It grew better as Katerina recovered from her ordeal in the jungle and Blade recovered from his wounds.

There was also the novelty of not being absolutely alone in Dimension X. Blade always managed to find friends and allies in any Dimension, people like Kordu. But there had never been anyone from Home Dimension before, anyone who knew that this world was not the only one, anyone who could sit and talk of England and France, London and Paris, jet planes and computers.

It was almost an idyll there in Thessu for Blade and Katerina, at least for a while. Crops slowly ripened under the sun, and parties of Hunters returned with trophies of meat or fish. Babies were born and tattooed with clan marks. Old men and women died and were cremated, and their ashes were buried or thrown into the rivers to return to the sources of all life and to be reborn. There were rumors that other peoples in the jungle and around it had learned of Geddo's death.

"This could mean war by next year," said Kordu. "Geddo was a cruel man and a dangerous enemy. But he was also a mighty leader in war. Now he is dead, and little is known of the new High Chief. The Ganthi have enemies who may wish to try their strength against us, now that Geddo no longer leads us."

"I have done better than Geddo once already," said

Blade. "With the aid of the gods I shall do better than he again." He did not feel quite that arrogant, but a High Chief had to strike the right poses! In any case, he would be long gone from among the Ganthi by next year.

What to do about Katerina, when he was called Home? On the one hand, if she returned with him she would be an enemy again, an enemy who knew dangerous secrets. On the other hand, if he deliberately left her here, her fate would be worse than he could wish even on a KGB agent. If she was left here to die, the secret of her successful trip to Dimension X would also die with her. Both personally and professionally, Blade rejected the idea of simply abandoning Katerina.

Could he repeat his success with Arllona with Katerina? That first time could have been sheer luck. Katerina was clearly far better able to make the trip. That didn't mean she would. He would try, when the time came. Once again, that wasn't enough, but it was all he could do.

With that decision out of the way, Blade was able to relax again. It was getting hard not to. This stay among the Ganthi felt at times more like a vacation than a trip to Dimension X.

The "vacation" did not last much longer. What brought it to an end was Drob-Log—"The Gods' Forge"—the great volcano in the mountains to the north that both Blade and Katerina had seen shortly after reaching this Dimension. The mountain had slept quietly since long before the oldest of the Ganthi could remember. Now it was awakening from that sleep. The three earthquakes at the time of Blade's defeat of Geddo had been the first sign.

The next sign was a new series of earthquakes. They were not strong at first, and once more there was little damage. They came frequently, though. For a solid week there was at least one a day.

Then there were two a day, and they grew stronger. People in Thessu began to wear haunted looks and to sleep outside at night, preferring the night damps and the insects to being caught in their collapsing houses. Then villagers from the north fled into the town, bringing tales that the smoke from the top of Drob-Log was turning from white to gray and rising higher and higher. that flames and liquid fire were appearing on the sides of the mountain. The gods were stoking up their forge.

Soon the cloud from the volcano rose high enough to dominate the northern horizon in Thessu itself. By night the base of the cloud glowed more fiercely every time Blade looked at it. He decided to go north and see Drob-Log in eruption with his own eyes. There was more than curiosity in this decision. A volcano that size could hurl ashes and deadly gas over hundreds of square miles of the hunting and farming lands of the Ganthi The whole life of the jungle and perhaps of the people could fall into confusion.

By the time Blade approached the base of the mountain, it was in full eruption. His escort would not go closer than ten miles, and he himself did not risk going closer than five. The mountain belched out gas and ashes in a continuous cloud that spread across half the sky, sent lava cascading down its side, and made the ground underfoot vibrate like the head of a drum. For miles below the tree line the jungle was already ash-covered and dying, and all the animal life had fled away to the south.

That wasn't the worst of it. Not only was Drob-Log wide awake now, some of its neighbors were also coming alive. Blade would have called all of them extinct. But by the time he and his grim-faced escort turned south, seven other mountains were spewing out dark clouds by day and fire by night. The stretch of dead or dying jungle was more than a day's march wide.

When Blade returned to Thessu, he knew there was only one safe thing to do. He put it into plain words before a gathering of all the Elder Brothers and clan heads.

"The gods are hard at work on *all* of their forges to the north. I counted seven, and there will be more. The mountains throw out ashes and cinders, like the ones from your cookfires, but so many that they bury the land as deep as a tall man's waist. They throw out evil vapors, like those that rise from a dead animal, but far worse. The vapors from the volcanoes will slay any who breathe them. The trees and the bushes, the grass and the crops of the Ganthi will die. The animals and the fish will die, or flee away to the south, away from the mountains."

"And the Ganthi?" That was Kordu, asking the question Blade had told him to ask.

"The Ganthi also will die if they do not flee away from the mountains, for in a year there may be nothing in all this land we call ours. Even if they stay, they will become so weak that their enemies may strike them down."

His voice rose. "If the Ganthi march forth, across the Great River and into the lands to the south, they will live. As they march they will be so strong that none may stop them, or keep them from taking as much land as they need to live. For we are the Ganthi, and others go in fear of us."

This appeal to the pride of the leaders did most of the work. The rest had already been done for him, by the earthquakes that by now had laid half of Thessu in ruins, and by the clouds to the north that grew more terrible each day. The warriors who had been with Blade were asked to speak, and they confirmed his tale of a land dead and still from the deadly breath of the mountains.

There was no discussion after that, and in fact no real need for it. They all knew that they must do as Blade urged, and after that there was nothing to do but scatter to their homes and start packing. It would be a long journey.

Blade went back to the High Chief's compound to warn the servants and the women. Then he and Katerina lay down and made love as fiercely as if they could somehow drive back the death that was stalking the jungle and its people.

Chapter Twenty

Moving all the Ganthi south of the Great River meant moving more than fifty thousand people across a hundred miles of jungle and hill. The Great River itself was a mile wide, with many rapids. Then there were the Gudki—the "Hairy People."

"We know only enough about them to know that they are dangerous," said Kordu. "They live mostly to the south of the Great River, but some of them cross it to hunt. They are no taller than the Ganthi, but they are much stronger and they have long brown hair all over their bodies. We kill them whenever we see them. They kill us whenever they can. That is not often, for they have only stone spears and axes. But they attack us often enough so that we call them an enemy to consider. They have great skill in laying ambushes."

Blade nodded. "We will have to think even more about them now. We are going to march all of the Ganthi right into their homeland."

In the end, Blade decided he would have to lead a scouting party to the south, searching out the best route for the great journey of the Ganthi. There would be no really "safe" route, but certainly some would be better than others.

Blade had enough volunteers for that scouting party to form a small army. He selected forty, including Katerina but not including Kordu. The man was not at all happy about this.

"It is not only my pride as a Hunter of the Ganthi that is hurt, Blade," he said quietly. "It is that I fear for you."

"Are the Gudki so dangerous, then?"

"No, but they are not the only enemies you may face. I have continued to listen as I promised you, and I have heard things I do not like. There are those who say that the gods have made the mountains burn because the Ganthi have done wrong to make a Stranger the High Chief."

"They can say what they please," replied Blade. "It will not make me less than High Chief, nor will it stop the mountains from burning."

"That is true," said Kordu. "But many are not wise. They might decide that the gods will make the mountains sleep again if you do not return from your journey to the south. Certainly that journey will give them an opportunity if they want one. I would be happier to go with you and do what a friend may do to guard your back."

"I honor you for this," said Blade, putting both hands on Kordu's shoulders. "But I say to you, and it is no shame to you, that my woman Katerina can do that also. You know well that she fights like a strong warrior."

"I do," said Kordu, with a reluctant smile.

"She can guard my back. She cannot do what I want you to do. I want you to stay here in Thessu, speak to all the Ganthi with my voice, tell them what to do and not to do until I return from the south. Will you do these things that Katerina cannot do?"

Kordu made all the gestures of respect and smiled widely. "I shall." Then he turned and left. Blade watched him go with relief. That was one considerable load off his mind. Kordu would be the best possible leader for the Ganthi while he himself scouted in the south. Besides, if something actually did happen to him—Gudki ambush, treachery, snakebite, fever, or anything else—Kordu would make a magnificent High Chief. The Ganthi would need good leadership to survive in their new homeland, and Kordu seemed like a man who could provide it.

Blade's leg was completely healed by the time the scouting party headed south from Thessu toward the Great River. He and Katerina were able to set a fast pace in the lead. The damp heat, the stinging insects, the vines that tangled and tripped feet were no more pleasant than before, but they didn't slow anyone down.

There seemed to be more wildlife around, though. It ranged from birds and creatures the size and shape of a housecat up to a pair of three-horns nearly as large as the one Blade had killed. Half the animals in the jungle seemed to be on the move, and all of them were heading south.

"Even the animals know what is going to happen in this land," said Katerina.

More than once the scouts had to stop and fight off monstrous reptiles. After they had lost half a dozen men in these fights, Blade ordered that from now on they would scatter or climb trees, rather than fight. The warriors and Hunters grumbled and muttered at this order. It went against all the traditions of the Ganthi and their own pride. But they obeyed.

About halfway to the Great River they saw their first signs of the Gudki. They practically stumbled over the long-haired, broad-framed corpse sprawled beside the path. It was already swollen and dark with decay, and large chunks of flesh had been slashed or torn out.

"They eat their own dead when they can find no other meat," said one of the Hunters.

The party moved on, with eyes searching even more carefully a forest that seemed even less friendly than before. When they camped that night Blade doubled the sentries, and they built screens of logs around their campfires to shield them from watching eyes.

After two more days it was clear that the Gudki were roaming the jungles in greater strength than ever before. They found more corpses—the victims of wild animals, snakes, or fallen trees. They found the ashes of campfires, and once they saw one glowing far off in the twilight. They found bloodstained hide garments, tufts of long gray hair, and half-eaten carcasses with stone spearpoints broken off in their death-wounds. The faces of the Ganthi grew strained and drawn. They had had much experience fighting the Gudki, but this was something new, something unknown. They were not yet ready to confess to being afraid, but they talked more freely to Blade.

"Only a few times have the Gudki come this far north of the Great River," the Hunters said. "Even when they did, they came only in twos and threes. They did not hunt, they did not build fires, they slipped through the forest unseen, like snakes. Now they must be coming here by the dozen. Many hundreds of them must be north of the river. The gods have chosen to play yet another trick on the Ganthi."

Blade shook his head. "It is not a new trick, but part of the same trick that makes the mountains burn. The mountains burn, and the animals run to the south. More animals means more meat for the Gudki than ever before. So to hunt this meat more of *them* come north of the river than ever before. That is all there is to it."

Blade knew he was right, but after a while he wasn't

sure he'd been right to say it. More often than before, he caught the Hunters and warriors looking strangely at him. He and Katerina started taking turns watching and sleeping at night. Early one morning, a spear thudded into a tree near where Blade lay asleep, missing Katerina by inches. It was a Gudki spear, yet there had been no signs of the Gudki all the day before and there were none the day after. Blade kept his mouth shut and his eyes even more wide open than before.

For two more days they marched through jungle that grew thinner by the hour, and at last they came out on the north bank of the Great River. It deserved the name. It stretched a mile from bank to bank, a mile of murky green water that swirled past as a frightening speed.

There were only two ways the Ganthi would get across it. Blade saw that at once. They could cross on rafts, which would take weeks. Or they could find a place where the river was shallow, and ford it. Even that would take time and much care, and they would certainly lose both people and animals. But it would take days rather than weeks.

Fords existed on the river—or so the stories said. Nobody seemed to know where any of them were, however. Blade decided to divide the scouting party in half, sending one group up the river and the other down it. Katerina wondered if it was wise to divide the scouts this way, with the Hairy People roaming the woods in such great numbers.

"Normally I'd agree with you," said Blade. "But we don't have much time." He pointed at the sky. Even this far south, the northern horizon was dark with the clouds from the volcanoes. "The ashes may already be falling on Thessu."

The scouting party camped that night on the north bank of the Great River, sentries out and alert. Three times they saw the faint flickering orange glows of Gudki campfires, far away in the darkness on the south bank. But the jungle around them was quiet.

The next morning the scouts split, and Blade and Katerina led their group down the river. They kept as close as they could to the bank all that day and the next, never losing sight of the water. Every few hundred yards they stopped and tested the depth of the water with poles. They found only one place where it was at all shallow enough, and there the bottom dropped off steeply a few hundred yards out.

They found signs of the Gudki in many places. Blade took care to make camp in places well clear of the trees, and he ordered that a third of the men should always be awake with spears in hand. They obeyed him without complaining. They might think him an offense against the gods, but no one wanted to end up as a meal for the Hairy People by defying him.

All of the third day they marched along a stretch of rapids where the river boiled whitely over great slabs of rock. It was dropping down through a range of heavily wooded hills, and Blade began to wonder if there was any possible crossing place for many days' march ahead. He didn't like the idea. Even if there was a ford far ahead, fifty thousand people could never march far into these hills to reach it.

Luck was with him, though. At about noon on the next day they reached a spot where the river broke its fall in a broad level stretch. The river ran fast there, so fast that the water was white with foam. But it also ran shallow, and the shallows seemed to extend clear across to the opposite bank. Blade waded out several hundred yards without finding water more than waist-deep.

The strong current would be a problem, of course. Just below the shallows an ugly stretch of rapids began. It would mean certain death for anyone swept off his feet and carried away downstream. Children, the old and sick, and the animals would have to be passed across almost from hand to hand. That would not be hard, though, since the bottom was firm.

Unless the party going upriver found something better, this was the ford. This was where the Ganthi would cross the Great River to their new homeland. That night Blade and Katerina slept soundly for the first time in several days.

The next morning Blade and Katerina led the scouts down to the bank and into the water. They had to make absolutely sure that the shallow water and the firm bottom extended clear across to the other bank. They were

132

all going, since Blade didn't want to divide the party again.

One by one the warriors and Hunters followed Blade and Katerina into the water. The shorter men staggered as the rushing water rose toward their chests. Their comrades grabbed their hands, their hair, their spears, anything to keep them from being swept away. Good luck and quick work kept anyone from being knocked down and carried off. Slowly but steadily, one cautious step at a time, they pushed across the foaming river toward the far bank.

Blade held one spear out at arm's length, probing the water ahead of him before taking each step. Behind him Katerina followed in his footsteps, spending most of her time looking back along the file of scouts. She watched to see that they kept up, and she also watched for any sort of trouble—a man swept away, or a spear coming at Blade's back.

Nothing happened. The shadows of the trees on the far bank reached slowly out across the water toward Blade. He scanned those trees carefully, searching for any sign of movement. He saw nothing, and once more the line moved forward.

Now the water bubbled and churned around Blade's knees. Then he was out of the main current, pushing through patches of scum and clots of dead leaves whirling slowly in eddies. He felt the bottom under his feet turn from gravel to mud, and he climbed up onto dry land. Katerina was just behind him. They stood back to back, Blade watching the forest, Katerina watching the river and the men climbing out of it. Two, three, four, five men followed them out onto dry land. Blade and Katerina moved a few yards inland, away from the bank.

The next scout was just climbing up onto the bank when a chorus of deep-throated howls split the air. A second later two well-thrown spears skewered the man. He screamed and fell backward into the water, one spear in his chest and another in his belly. The next scout and all those behind him froze where they were.

It was a well-laid ambush by the Gudki. Before Blade could do more than turn around, more than fifty of the Hairy People came swarming out of the jungle. They

133

leaped down from the branches, sprang out from behind trees and under bushes, came running along the bank. The ones who ran along the bank dashed in between Blade and the men still in the water. Clubs thudded, iron and stone spearheads drove into living flesh, cries of rage and agony exploded. Several scouts and a dozen Gudki went down in the first minute, writhing and choking in their own blood. Blade found himself and Katerina and three of the scouts being forced away from the bank, toward the jungle.

That could mean disaster. Surrounded, they could and would be overwhelmed and cut down by sheer weight of numbers. Blade smashed a spear butt into the face of an attacker, shouted to Katerina to guard his back, and turned to shout to the men still in the water. If those men pushed forward through the Gudki, Blade and his group could still make a safe retreat.

The men were not pushing forward, to close with the Gudki or do anything else. They were moving hastily away, out into the river, out of range of Gudki spears and away from any chance of helping Blade.

Blade cursed them at the top of his lungs. If he hadn't needed his spears he would have thrown them at the retreating men. They weren't retreating in panic or fear, either. They were splashing away in good order, spears on their shoulders, not even looking back at the fight on the bank. They were abandoning him and Katerina and their comrades to the Gudki. They were abandoning the High Chief who had brought down the wrath of the gods on the Ganthi.

One of the men looked back, hesitated, then turned as if he wanted to change his mind. Instantly three of his comrades rammed their spears into his stomach. He doubled over, lost his footing, and went bobbing away downriver as the current caught him. A trail of blood followed him. Obviously the men in the water had their story all worked out, about how they had been driven away from the High Chief after a valiant fight. They were ready to kill anyone who might tell a different story. Grimly Blade turned back to fight the Gudki as long as he could stay on his feet.

Another of the scouts had gone down while Blade was watching the men in the river. A second tried to make a break toward the bank, through the Gudki and into the water. He leaped at the enemy, screaming wildly and flourishing both spears until they blurred in the air. Three Gudki went down before him, dead or dying. Half a dozen more stood between him and safety. Five of them scattered, the sixth closed and grappled him, nails like claws digging into his skin. The scout screamed even louder than before, dropped his own spears, and clamped his hands on the enemy's throat. The fighters toppled over, rolled to the bank, and slid into the water with a tremendous splash, still locked together. They rose to the surface once, in a tangle of thrashing limbs, then sank for good.

The man's suicidal charge drew the Gudki's attention away from Blade and Katerina for a moment giving them and the last scout just time enough to form a triangle, all three facing outward, each with a spear in one hand and a club in the other.

Then the Gudki came at them from all sides, masses of heavy-bodied hairy men. Their howls deafened Blade, the reek of their breath and matted hair stifled him, their spears and clubs whistled at him and around him. All Blade could do was to tell friend from enemy and desperately try to meet each enemy as he came at him.

Club down an arm reaching to grab his belt. Run his spear into a hairy throat in time to make a blow at his head only graze an ear. Draw the spear back and thrust low to pin to the ground an already crippled enemy crawling in to grab him by the ankles. Listen to a hoarse death-scream rise above the uproar and echo around the forest. A spearpoint coming in? Beat it aside with the club, so hard that the spearshaft snaps in two and the stone point flies off like an arrow. But the enemy comes on, raising his shaft like a club. That courage is wasted—a quick thrust takes the attacker in the stomach. He doubles over, trying to hold his own guts inside him, until a club smashes down on his head. Then he kicks out his life at Blade's feet, just in time to let another of the Gudki leap into the attack over the body.

How long it went on, Blade couldn't even guess. All he knew was that it went on and on and on, a steady orgy of killing, with Katerina and the last scout doing their share on either side of him. It went on until suddenly the scout was down, blood spurting from a fatally gashed thigh. Blade braced himself to face a final, overwhelming charge and go down fighting. Then he realized that the way to the rear was open. They were no longer surrounded. He nudged Katerina, and slowly they backed away, blood-caked spears and clubs still raised.

There were still more than fifty of the Gudki in sight. More must have come out of the forest during the fight. Nearly as many lay dead or dying in a wide belt from the edge of the jungle down to the river bank. Their blood turned the earth into red mud and their dying groans and whimpers drowned out the sound of the river. It was a couple of minutes before the Gudki started forward over the bodies of their comrades.

Blade and Katerina backed away before the advancing line of Gudki. As the enemy came on, they stretched to the right, more and more of them slipping between Blade and the river.

Blade fought down a temptation to turn and run for the jungle. His experience told him that the Gudki would charge the moment he and Katerina turned their backs.

The slow retreat down the bank went on. The roar of the river sounded louder. At first Blade thought it was nothing but the silence after the battle that made the river sound louder. Then he realized that they must be approaching the rapids.

Blade began to see mist rising above the bank. The roar grew louder. Slowly the Gudki began to edge away from the bank, closer to Blade. He sensed a moment approaching, a moment when the fragile truce would collapse as the Gudki swept in from both sides.

Instead he heard a sudden hoarse scream. Two of the Gudki waved their long arms desperately, then vanished as a soft portion of the bank crumbled under them. They screamed again as they plunged downward. Blade could just hear the faint splashes above the swelling thunder of the rapids.

The other Gudki along the riverbank scattered as if the earth under their feet had suddenly turned red-hot. They gabbled and growled, waved their spears and gestured to each other. For a moment they seemed to forget that Blade and Katerina existed.

In that moment Blade estimated the distance to the river bank, knew that the two of them could make it, and saw that this was their best chance. Death in the water was likely, but it would be cleaner than certain death under Gudki spears, especially for Katerina. He caught her by one arm, pointed with the other hand toward the bank, and pushed her. She dashed toward the rising wall of mist, with Blade three steps behind her.

They reached the bank almost together. As they did, the Gudki awoke from their shock, realized that their prey was escaping, and let out howls that drowned out the river. If they'd thrown a few spears as well as just howling, they might still have scored. In the moment the Gudki wasted making noise, Blade and Katerina looked down and saw the water boiling past far below in the mist. They could only hope their landing place would be deep enough and free of rocks. Then they threw their weapons aside and plunged out and down into the misty air.

Chapter Twenty-One

The foam-flecked water leaped up at them out of the mist. It seemed to lash every inch of Blade's skin with burning-cold whips as it swallowed him. He plunged deep, so deep that there was darkness around him even when he opened his eyes. Then the rocks of the river bottom swept up out of the darkness at him. Blade stretched out both arms, caught himself on his hands, and pushed away from the bottom. As he pushed, the current caught him and swept him up and away.

He had to struggle up toward the light and the surface. At each moment he became more certain his lungs would explode before he made it. Then his head broke surface. He sucked in a great gasping breath of air, nearly strangled as a wave broke over him, then started swimming furiously. The river roared in his ears and rocks seemed to be rushing past at the speed of an express train. But he did not go under again.

Blade was several hundred yards downstream before he spotted Katerina's soaked blond head rising on the crest of a wave. He signalled to her, narrowly missed being cut in two by a razor-edged spire of rock, then saw her wave back. She was swimming strongly, and he began stroking his way toward her as fast as the river would let him.

Time after time Blade would swim ten feet toward Katerina, then a sudden surge of water would carry him twenty feet back. Once he skidded over a large rock on his chest and belly, scraping himself painfully, then he plunged safely into the water beyond. He was almost within speaking distance of her when the river suddenly dropped ten feet straight down. They both went under, deep into the dark pool at the base of the drop. Blade broke surface first, wondered if Katerina had survived, then saw her rise almost beside him. She had half a dozen minor wounds from the battle with the Gudki, and she was bleeding from a cut along the jaw. Otherwise she seemed unhurt, and was swimming strongly as the current took them again and swept them out of the pool, on down the river.

The next stretch of rapids was less wild than the first. Blade had time to look along the banks, searching for a place to climb out. They were certainly miles downstream from the Gudki now. They were probably beyond the farthest point the scouts had reached in exploring the river bank. The roaring river was sweeping them away into the unknown.

The river was less savage here, but the banks were even more inhospitable. They rose in walls of fissured, seamed rock, a hundred feet or more straight up to craggy skylines. High above, Blade saw patches of blue sky through the swirling mist. Once he saw the fleeting silhouette of a bird. Otherwise they seemed to be passing through a lifeless land, with nothing around them but cold water and bare rock. The current was still too fast to let them reach for handholds, and how would they climb the cliffs even if they somehow got out of the water? There was nothing to do except ride the river down through the canyon and hope for the best.

Blade began to lose track of time in the water. He had to fight to be aware of Katerina as she swam along beside him. He had to fight to be aware of rocks and whirlpools ahead. He had to fight to be aware of anything except the roar of the water in his ears and the bitter chill that slowly worked its way up his arms and legs.

They would have to get out of this water soon. Otherwise the cold would become the ally of the current. Too numb to swim, they would be swept under or smashed and mangled against the rocks. Blade forced himself to look ahead and to either side, hoping for some break in the walls of the canyon. He saw nothing—no ledges, no handholds, nothing but looming faces of gray rock that a monkey couldn't have climbed.

More time passed, and the current began to speed up again. Waves heaved them up and down now, foam-crested waves that rose ten or fifteen feet up the walls of the canyon. Blade found that his arms and legs would no longer move exactly where he wanted them or as fast as he wanted them to. The roar of the water rose again until a bomb could have gone off unheard. Blade could not hope to make Katerina hear a single word, but he could see her face clearly, only a few feet away. Her skin was as pale as a fish's belly, and her hair trailed like seaweed behind her. Her face was set and strained, eyes half-closed. Cold and exhaustion were creeping up on her, too.

In Kano, he and Arllona had escaped from death by fire. Now, here in the land of the Ganthi, it looked as though he and Katerina might very well die by water.

Far below the Tower of London, J sat on the little folding seat and watched Lord Leighton readying the computer. In another few moments the sequence would begin for returning Blade from Dimension X. J's eyes shifted from the computer and its master to the chair in its glass booth. In another few minutes after that Blade should materialize in the chair, or at least near it. Then J could breathe more easily, at least until the time came for Blade to be hurled off into the unknown again.

An idea struck J. He turned it over and over in his mind until he thought he could put it into words without its sounding like a joke. Lord Leighton would be in no mood to appreciate jokes now.

"Leighton," he said. "What about Katerina?"

The scientist turned and his bushy white eyebrows rose inquiringly. "Could you be more precise, please?"

"Have you considered the possibility of her being returned to Home Dimension along with Blade?"

Leighton looked severe. "Of course." His tone implied that it was at least mildly insulting to even imply that he hadn't considered this and a host of even less likely possibilities. "I think that's a rather low-order probability. To be sure of bringing two people back from Dimension X, we would need two separate Recall Modules. Each one would have to be programmed with the brain pattern of the individual being recalled. I doubt if the expense of a second Recall Module would be justified unless and until we have a second person out in Dimension X whom we want to bring back."

J suppressed a grin. This was the first time he could recall in the whole history of Project Dimension X that Leighton had been *opposed* to spending money on the computer.

"In point of fact," Leighton went on, "it's not theoretically impossible for the computer to affect Katerina, assuming she's still alive and sane."

"A rather large assumption," put in J.

"True. But if her brain is functioning, it will be more susceptible to Recall than any other brain in Dimension X except Blade's. If the Recall pattern coincides with a receptive pattern in her brain, we may at least haul her out of the Dimension where she is now."

J nodded, but his mind was leaping ahead to a disturbing possibility. "Is there any danger to Blade in that?"

Leighton cocked his head on one side as he considered his answer. "There's always the chance of unexpected results when the pattern of Recall varies from the norm. I wouldn't care to predict whether or not these results could mean danger to Blade." Then, seeing J's grim look, he added more cheerfully, "If I had to—ah, guess—I would say no."

"Thank you." J was genuinely grateful. He knew

what an effort of will it took for the scientist to make a guess, and then to *admit* it.

Leighton turned back to the main control panel. "Ah—very good. The sequence is running smoothly." He looked up at the timer clock above the panel. The second hand was sweeping up around the dial, toward the vertical.

It reached the vertical. A green light flashed on over the red master switch. Leighton's hand closed on the switch, then slammed it down to the bottom of its slot.

There was a thump and a crash that echoed around the chamber and made the floor heave. There was an enormous sizzling sound, like a thousand eggs dropped all at once onto a hot grill. J smelled smoke, and by pure reflex he threw himself flat on the floor.

Then all the lights went out.

The pain began so gently this time that Blade at first thought it was just an earache from the cold water. It faded away almost entirely after the first pulse. Then it returned, strong, sharp, and unmistakable. The computer was reaching out to grip his mind; now was the moment to see if he could make it grip Katerina's as well.

He lunged through the water at her as the pain swelled. He reached out and grabbed her by one hand. As he did, she screamed out loud and turned her face toward him. Her eyes were closed and her mouth twisted in pain. She gasped and moaned, "My head—it hurts—I—"

Blade burst out in a shout of surprise and delight. The computer was reaching Katerina too, gripping her brain without any help from him, ready to drag her back! He still reached out to her, putting an arm across her shoulders and turning her around. She screamed again and clutched wildly at him. Her arms went around him and her nails dug into his skin. She was forgetting the river, the current, the rocks—everything except the pain in her head.

A moment later the explosion came in Blade's own skull. He felt his vision going, felt the coldness and the pressure of the water against his skin fading, threw his own arms around Katerina. It seemed to him that they

141

were now sweeping upward to the brink of a great black cliff, the mist boiling around them, blue and green and red light sparking and flashing all around.

They almost reached the top of the cliff. As Blade reached out for the black rock, the light flared around them again and they began to fall. He felt Katerina slipping away from him, clutched her more tightly than before, felt her warmth against him. Wrapped around each other as closely as they had ever been in their love-making, Blade and Katerina fell down through the mists and the flashing lights.

In the darkness of the computer room, J rose to his feet. He took a step forward, felt something roll out from under his foot, and fell sprawling. He groped around for what had tumbled him, got a grip on it, and laughed. It was exactly what the situation called for—the emergency hand torch, thrown down from its bracket by the explosion. J switched on the light and stood up again.

He wouldn't have been surprised to see the computer a mass of smoking wreckage, with Leighton's charred corpse tangled among blackened wires and twisted metal. He was relieved to see that whatever had happened hadn't done that. The air in the room was faintly hazed with smoke, and all the lights on the consoles were out. Everything else looked the same as before, including Lord Leighton.

The scientist was sitting on the floor, shaking his head and looking slightly dazed. As the light fell on him he blinked and tried to get to his feet. J stepped over and helped him rise. Leighton brushed himself off and the two men exchanged looks.

"What the devil happened?" asked J.

Leighton looked toward the chair in its booth. "We don't seem to have either Blade or Katerina back at the moment. Otherwise, I'd rather defer an answer until we have more data."

J did not much care for that answer. In plain language, it meant that Lord Leighton didn't have the remotest notion of what had happened, or very much hope of finding out any time soon.

As Blade came awake, the first thing he felt was the warm weight of Katerina on him. That didn't surprise him. They'd been swept out of Dimension X locked in each other's arms, so there was no reason why they shouldn't have landed back in Home Dimension the same way.

Except—he felt short, damp grass against his bare skin. A deep roaring sounded in his ears. Blade opened his eyes and saw overhead a dark, star-spangled sky—and to one side, a great, raw, pulsing orange glow.

Blade tried to rise and found that Katerina was only half-conscious and weighing him down. Gently he rolled her off onto the grass that shouldn't have been there and lurched to his feet. His head whirled with pain and dizziness. For a moment he wasn't sure he could control his legs or his stomach. Then his head and vision cleared.

He took one look around him, and now his head whirled with surprise. What he saw should have been impossible. But it was true. So he wouldn't waste time denying it or doubting it.

He and Katerina had not returned to Home Dimension. Somehow they'd been caught up by the computer, whirled through the unknown that lay between Dimensions, and dropped back in Kano! Kano, the city of black jade and the Consecrated, the city of the Mouth of the Gods where he and Arllona had been about to burn, the city under siege by the Raufi of the desert. Kano, where he had been a prisoner condemned to sacrifice in the Mouth of the Gods. He could not be far from the Mouth either, not with that orange glow in the sky.

Blade took another look. He certainly wasn't far from the Mouth of the Gods! He was standing behind the First Consecrated's viewing stand, less than a hundred yards from the flames. What was even worse, he recognized the two tall, lean figures silhouetted against the glow on top of the stand.

They were Tyan, the First Consecrated, and Mirdon, the Commander Tyan had chosen to watch Blade's death with him.

Blade shook his head. This seemed even more impossible than what had already happened. Yet it was just

143

as undeniably true. He had not only returned to Kano, he had returned to Kano at the very time and place of his own sacrifice!

Chapter Twenty-Two

"This is getting bloody ridiculous," Blade said to himself.

That was putting it mildly. He really didn't have words strong enough to express what he felt. If he'd had Lord Leighton at hand, there would have been a few pointed questions. Lord Leighton was still a long way off, though, and—

At this point someone among the soldiers and slaves watching the sacrifice noticed the two people who had suddenly appeared behind the Consecrated's viewing stand. They had no business being there. Several men shouted angrily. Then there was a general rush toward Blade, the soldiers drawing their swords as they ran.

Blade dropped into fighting stance and got ready to grab the sword of the first soldier who came at him. He was damned sure that this time he could and would force the Kanoans to kill him! He was not going to let things end up this time with him and Katerina tied onto the grill and pushed foot by foot into the Mouth of the Gods.

The leading soldiers promptly stopped and the ones behind crashed into them. Half a dozen soldiers went sprawling on the ground. They picked themselves up but didn't come any closer.

Blade realized that he must appear a weird, even monstrous figure—a huge man, naked, bearded, suntanned, scarred, crouching there in fighting stance. It was even possible that no one would recognize him as he was now. He might be able to pass himself off as someone newly come to Kano, a strong fighter who could help against the Raufi. There wasn't much chance of that—the Kanoans were too nervous, too suspicious. But there *was* a small chance, and Katerina's being with him would help. She was several inches taller than Arllona,

144

and as blond as the other woman had been dark. No one could confuse the two.

Blade rose from fighting stance and spread out both hands in the traditional gesture of peace. "I come to Kano in peace," he said, raising his voice to be heard over the roar of the Mouth of the Gods.

"There is no peace in Kano!" shouted someone angrily, raising a pistol. Light glinted on its barrel. Blade shifted position, ready to shield Katerina and charge in if the bullet missed or didn't cripple him.

The pistol was raised and ready, but the bullet never came. Instead, a voice cut through the angry babble of the crowd, drowning it out, beating it down, rising even above the roar of the Mouth of the Gods.

"Hold your hands, you fools! Would you defy the gods, here at their very Mouth? Stand away and let me judge this matter."

It was Tyan's voice. The note of command in it was unmistakable. Blade's eyes followed the tall figure of the First Consecrated as he came down the stairs from the viewing stand and walked slowly around toward Blade and Katerina. Tyan's three trumpeters ran to escort him, trumpets slung over their backs and swords drawn. He didn't need them. His manner alone was enough to clear a path for him. Slaves and soldiers backed away hastily and knelt down as Tyan approached Blade.

Blade had seldom found it as difficult to keep calm as he did now under Tyan's examination. Tyan gave the impression of seeing and knowing everything about Blade without letting Blade see or know anything about him. It was hard to believe that those enormous dark eyes were not seeing through Blade's beard and sunburn, recognizing him for what he was. It was impossible to tell. Blade was just as glad that Katerina was still only half-conscious. She was in no shape to cope with this merciless examination. He wondered how much longer it would go on, and what Tyan would say when he'd finished.

Moments later, Blade got his answer. Tyan's arms shot up, making the sleeves of his robe billow out like great wings. For a moment he looked like some huge, grotesque bird about to take flight. Then his voice rose again, even louder than before. There was still a note of command in it, but there was also awe and ecstasy and the thrill of announcing an enormous discovery.

"Oh, people of Kano—behold the Champion of the Gods! In our time of need the gods have heard our prayers. They have sent a Champion to lead us with his strength. A woman comes with him to lend us her wisdom.

"Hail the Champion of the Gods!

"Hail the woman of the Champion!

"Hail the new day that dawns for Kano!

"Hail the downfall and doom of the Raufi! Their false god can no longer aid them, for the true gods have spoken. All hail the Champion of the Gods! Hail! Hail! Hail!"

Tyan rested a hand on Blade's shoulder and drew him forward to where the soldiers and slaves could see him more clearly. They began to join in the shouts of "Hail! Hail to the Champion of the Gods!"

Tyan stepped closer to Blade and started to go down on his knees. As his mouth passed close to Blade's ear, Blade heard the First Consecrated say in a low, urgent whisper:

"Keep your face straight and play this out if you want to live to die in bed."

Blade badly wanted to break out laughing instead. He stepped forward and raised both arms over his head as Tyan knelt on the grass before him. The shouts grew louder. People began running from all around the amphitheater to see what was going on. They too knelt as they saw Tyan kneeling before Blade, and their voices joined the uproar.

The crowd swelled steadily until there must have been five hundred people—soldiers, slaves, servants, the Consecrated themselves—crowding around Blade and Tyan. All of them were shouting at the top of their lungs, in the grip of a total hysterical adoration of the Champion of the Gods. They were beginning to give Blade another headache.

Eventually Tyan lifted his head to meet Blade's eyes and nodded slightly. Blade returned the nod. Tyan rose to his feet and gestured to quiet the crowd. Bit by bit the noise died away. When he could make himself heard, Tyan shouted, "People! Go forth from this place, and tell all you meet—the Champion of the Gods is come to Kano! Tell all you meet to take heart, aim true, smite the Raufi with greater strength, for Kano shall live!"

The cheers and the shouting exploded deafeningly all over again. Meanwhile Blade was bending over Katerina. To his relief she seemed to be awake and aware now, if still a little dizzy. He was helping her to her feet when Tyan came over to them and again spoke to Blade. The crowd was shouting so hysterically that this time he didn't need to whisper.

"If you help Kano live, my friend, so shall you. Otherwise—" Blade nodded. Tyan smiled thinly. The understanding between them was clear, and for the moment that was all they needed. The details could come later.

Tyan motioned his three trumpeters to clear a path. They complied, with trumpet calls and flourishes of their swords. As the path opened for them, Tyan led Blade and Katerina down it, away from the Mouth, away from the crowd, away into darkness and silence.

Chapter Twenty-Three

An hour later three heavily excorted sedan chairs delivered Tyan, Blade, and Katerina to the House of the Consecrated in the heart of the inner city. By that time, the rumor of the Champion's coming was running about the whole city. So were thousands of men and women, shouting, screaming, weeping in hysterical joy and relief and religious frenzy, waving torches and swords, letting off guns, broaching wine barrels, and generally making as much noise as the Raufi could have done in sacking the city.

Blade's head was throbbing and Katerina looked half-dead again. Tyan looked as tough and unruffled as ever. Blade had the impression that the First Consecrated would stay calm if the earth was threatening to open up and swallow him or the sky was about to fall down on his head.

Tyan did not relax until the three of them were locked in the innermost of his private chambers in the House of the Consecrated. The furnishings were austere,

147

almost monkish. Tyan was apparently a man who took his vows of asceticism seriously.

"It gives little comfort to the body," the man said, as he noticed Blade looking around. "But it is altogether proof against prying ears, and that gives much comfort to the spirit now. All the servants who enter here are deaf-mutes, and no others enter unless I know them to be absolutely trustworthy."

"I do not suppose you include Jormin on the list of the trustworthy," said Blade.

Again Tyan smiled thinly. His face did not seem designed for broad smiles, grins, or laughter. "By custom it is the right of the Second Consecrated to enter the private chambers of the First. It is also the right of the First to ignore custom when there is good reason for it. Does that answer your question?

"It does."

"Good. Now—do you wish a drink?" Blade nodded. "Good. Anything that may be found in Kano can be prepared. I shall summon a servant."

Tyan drank plain water, while Blade and Katerina took a light chilled white wine. As they drank, Blade had a chance to look more closely at the First Consecrated. The man was older than he'd suspected, closer to sixty than fifty. Now that he was no longer on public display, he also looked tired. Those deep eyes were red with fatigue, and there were nets of wrinkles in their corners and on the high forehead and scalp.

When all three had emptied their cups, Tyan smiled a third time. "I will not waste time wondering how you escaped from the very jaws of the Mouth of the Gods. You did it. That is sufficient for the moment. It is even more useful that your new woman disguised you so carefully that no one but myself appears to have recognized you. That was a remarkable feat in a very short time, incidentally. My compliments to you, my lady." He raised his cup in salute to Katerina. She managed a faint smile.

"I shall be interested in hearing more of how you did these things, after the Raufi are no longer camped outside the walls. For the moment, though, you are the Champion of the Gods and we will all be much too busy."

"I rather imagine so," said Blade. "What precisely am I supposed to do?"

Tyan set his cup down and straightened up. "First, keep your mouth shut. I do not fear the people. By morning they will be so ready to believe in the Champion of the Gods that they will go on believing and never doubt, no matter what you say. But there are people like Jormin and his supporters among the Consecrated. There are also the Jade Masters. They could have reasons for doubting you, so do and say nothing to strengthen such doubts."

"I shall be careful," said Blade. He remembered what Arllona had told him, about the Jade Masters' possible willingness to betray Kano in return for their own safety. Should he mention that now? No, it wasn't the right time. Besides, the coming of the "Champion of the Gods" might keep the Jade Masters loyal, or at least quiet. He would keep his eyes and ears open, but for the moment he would keep his mouth shut about the Jade Masters.

"Second," went on Tyan, "show yourself to the Consecrated and the people, so that everyone may know that you have truly come. That will start tomorrow morning, and I am afraid it will go on for a very long time. I do not ask you to enjoy being on display like a clown or a performing bear. I ask, however, that you endure it."

Blade grinned. "I appreciate your concern, Tyan. It shall be as you say. I wish to live—and I wish Kano to live, also."

Again the thin smile. "I am happy to hear that you can say that, whether you believe it or not. Say it again tomorrow morning, before the Consecrated, and before every other audience you may find in Kano. There are too many who believe that the gods have judged us and found us unworthy to survive. Such may not turn traitor, but they will hardly fight as well as they must if we are to be saved."

"I shall." There was something almost refreshing in Tyan's cool cynicism. It was certainly a contrast to the superstitious fears of the Ganthi that had so nearly killed both him and Katerina.

Tyan rose. "I can think of nothing else at the moment, but feel free to make suggestions. Now, however, it is time to begin preparing for the audience with the Consecrated. It will be at dawn, as custom orders."

Blade was tempted to suggest what Tyan could do with custom. He badly wanted to go off somewhere and sleep, and Katerina looked about ready to fall flat on her face with sheer exhaustion.

Yet it would never do for the Champion of the Gods or his woman to show any common mortal weaknesses so soon. Blade suppressed a sigh and nodded. "Tell us what to do, and we shall do it."

The grand presentation of the Champion of the Gods to the Consecrated of Kano took place on schedule. Blade and Katerina stood on a dais in the High Chamber of the House of the Consecrated. Four of the senior Consecrated held a purple canopy trimmed with gold over them. Katerina wore a long white robe and a small gold circlet in her hair. Blade wore a larger circlet set with jewels. Otherwise he was naked except for a jeweled loinguard and a sword. He was bathed and oiled and perfumed, he looked magnificent and inspiring, and he felt thoroughly ridiculous. But his own life and Katerina's, and perhaps the safety of Kano as well, depended on his playing his part, so he knew he would keep a straight face if it killed him!

Fortunately, Tyan kept his presentation short. He didn't have to whip up the Consecrated to a pitch of religious hysteria. They did the job themselves. They howled and shrieked and sobbed in ecstasy. Tyan had to station his three trumpeters around the dais with long staves, or the Consecrated might have scrambled up onto it and mobbed the Champion. It was clear that none of the Consecrated doubted Tyan's story, or Blade's truly being the Champion of the Gods. These people desperately wanted to believe in Blade, and in the kindness of gods who had sent him to Kano at the last moment.

Blade felt much easier in his mind about the whole affair after seeing his reception by the Consecrated. Physically, he still felt ready to drop, and Katerina stumbled and swayed as she walked along beside him. On top of everything else, they'd had to do the whole ceremony on empty stomachs. Fasting was also part of the custom.

Eventually they were left alone, in a room with a large canopied bed and a large table completely covered with silver dishes of food. For a little while Blade wasn't sure what he should do first. Hunger won out. He helped Katerina to a chair, sat down, and passed her the first dish that came to hand. Somehow she managed to find the strength to pick up knife and spoon and begin eating.

Food and wine made both of them feel clearheaded and alert enough to talk. There was no way Blade could avoid admitting to Katerina that he'd been in this Dimension before, so he didn't try. After a while he found himself telling her most of what had happened to him the first time he had been in Kano.

Once again, they were in a clear-cut survival situation. Katerina's knowing what had happened could endanger the security of the Project. On the other hand, her *not* knowing could endanger both of them, here and now. Speaking frankly was by far the more sensible solution.

Katerina didn't seem to have any trouble following his story. By now she was probably getting more or less used to the incredible happening to her or to Blade. She asked a few questions, but for the most part listened in silence. When Blade had finished, however, she nodded and spoke.

"The Second Consecrated—Jormin—was he the one on the right front of the canopy?"

Blade nodded. "I suppose Tyan made him stand there to teach him humility."

Katerina laughed, but without amusement. "That is a man who will never learn humility. I do not think it was wise to put him so close to us."

"Do you think he recognized me?"

"He was not looking at you, Blade. He was looking at me. I did not like the way he was looking."

"How was that?"

"It is not a way you would recognize, Blade. You are a man. Jormin has the look of a man who has suddenly become obsessed with a woman. A sick look. I—I have seen it before. It will make him a terrible enemy to you, that the woman he wants is yours."

The KGB was notoriously full of psychopaths. Blade was quite sure that Katerina was telling the truth when she said she'd seen that look before. Was she telling the truth about having seen it in Jormin? She might be. The man was mad enough for practically anything.

Katerina went on. "I think—I think that if I let him speak to me—he might say what is in his mind. If he plans anything against us, I can learn it. If he does not, then that is one less thing we have to think about."

Yes, thought Blade. You could also tell him who I really am, and get me killed off. Again he balanced risks. Katerina might try to betray him. But would even Jormin believe her? If she was believed, she would probably involve herself in his downfall. The Kanoans, enraged at the betrayal of their hopes, would kill her as well as Blade.

She might also do exactly what she was promising. Why not, in fact? She must know enough about the Project by now to realize that sooner or later they would be returning to England. If they returned together, she could hope that he would save her from immediate execution. That in turn, respite, could give her a chance to escape or get her information out later. If he died here and she somehow survived to return to Home Dimension, she might be killed the minute she appeared in the chair at the complex. She certainly would have no chance to escape or to send out information. J would see to that.

Blade kept turning the question over and over in his mind, and slowly realized what was making it hard for him to decide.

He did not want to believe that Katerina *would* betray him. He was not quite in danger of falling in love with a KGB agent. He *was* losing some of his professional detachment where Katerina was concerned. For a long time now they had shared dangers, protected each other, and made love. It was becoming hard to remember that Katerina had been an enemy and could become one again.

She would not become an enemy here in Kano. That was his answer and his decision, for better or for worse.

Blade reached toward the wine jug, to refill his cup and Katerina's. He was interrupted by a soft thud and a gentle snore. He looked to see that Katerina's head had sagged forward onto the table. Her hair was trailing over the remains of a chicken. He sprang up, ready to shout for help, then she snored again. Blade laughed. Katerina was sound asleep, and nothing more.

That was hardly surprising. It was high time they both got some sleep. He bent down, lifted Katerina gently, and carried her off toward the bed.

The sign on the door to his chamber said that Jormin was Meditating. Inside the chamber the Second Consecrated sat on the ceremonial rug, in the correct posture, his eyes closed. Anyone seeing him would have called him a model of devoutness, assuming his inner vision to be fixed upon the gods and their wisdom.

Actually, his inner vision was fixed upon the blond woman who had come to Kano with the man Tyan called Champion of the Gods. He saw her as he wanted her, sprawled naked on the floor of his cell, bruises and welts dark on her pale flesh, doing his bidding, begging and whimpering for the chance to do his bidding.

He would cheerfully have gone into the Mouth of the Gods afterward if he could have made that vision a reality, even once.

Fortunately, there was no need to pay such a price. Others would pay it for him. Others—the people of Kano. If he could deliver the city to Dahrad Bin Saffar and the Raufi, surely—surely they would deliver the woman to him. The woman, and at least some of the power he had always dreamed of wielding.

It would stay a dream now, unles he struck hard and soon. How Tyan had managed this travesty, this "Champion of the Gods" spectacular, Jormin did not know or care. He did know that the First Consecrated had made his position utterly secure by it. Perhaps Tyan could even cast down the Second Consecrated. It was some three hundred years since that had happened, but a First Consecrated who could claim to have the gods in his pocket could do much. Jormin trembled, with fear as well as with desire for the blond woman.

He could not yield up Kano singlehanded, of course. He would need the help of the Jade Masters, and doubtless they would demand a share in the rule of Kano after the Raufi came. They wouldn't demand the woman, however. Anything else they could have, and perhaps in time he could find ways of easing them out of even that.

The Jade Masters would not give him that help unless he asked. Even in the asking there was some risk. Tyan's spies were everywhere, and what Tyan's spies did not see, Mirdon's might catch. Yet the alternative was to abandon all hope of the woman, and to sit quietly until Tyan chose to strike him down.

He would not do that, not when he could so easily avoid it.

Chapter Twenty-Four

The coming of the Champion of the Gods touched off three days of hysteria in Kano. It was all Mirdon and the other commanders could do to keep the walls patrolled and the troops disciplined.

Eventually the uproar died down. The people of Kano awoke with monumental hangovers, to realize that the Raufi still had their city under siege. The Champion of the Gods had come, but the Raufi had not gone.

"In fact, we're almost worse off than before," Mirdon said to Blade one evening as they stood on the outer wall. The campfires of the Raufi gleamed ominously in the darkness only two miles away. "All the food that got eaten up in the celebrations these past few days is food we'll miss before long. The Raufi aren't going to lift the siege simply because you've come, and as long as they stay here we're cut off."

Either someone had told Mirdon Blade's secret, or the man had guessed it himself. But he knew how important keeping that secret was for Kano, and he held his tongue. He spoke to Blade as one experienced soldier to another. That put both of them at ease. Blade quickly found himself both liking and respecting Mirdon.

"Besides," Mirdon went on, "everyone is going to think each Kanoan is now worth ten of the Raufi, because the gods are on our side. I know that isn't true, you know that isn't true, but do the people, the common soldiers, know it? They don't. That means before long they'll be clamoring to be led out against the Raufi. If we listen to that clamor, they'll be butchered and the Raufi can walk in over the bodies. If we don't yield, they'll start clamoring for my head at least, and sooner or later for yours and Tyan's. Then we'll have civil war in Kano, and the Raufi will be certain to find someone willing to let them through the gates."

Mirdon looked along the walls, with their cannon-armed towers and their helmeted musketeers. "If the Raufi would make an attack on the walls now, we could butcher them. We've got all the men and guns and powder we need. Everyone will fight like tigers with the Champion's eye on them. Their inexperience won't matter. All they'll have to do is stand or die, and they can and will do that.

"But if Dahrad Bin Saffar has half the brains he must have to have done all that he's done, he won't order an attack. The Raufi will sit out there and wait. They can wait longer than we can, and eventually they'll win."

Mirdon sighed and turned back to Blade with a bitter smile on his long face. "Champion, I don't hold this against you. You've done much and you'll do more, and I'm sure in the end you'll die gallantly with us. But one miracle isn't enough. We'll need another one to save Kano."

Blade spent a good part of his time during the next few days wandering around Kano, inspecting the fighters. He discovered that Mirdon was quite right. With enough food and ammunition, the city could hold out for any length of time. Unfortunately, it would be out of both within a month or two.

Those who knew this were carefully keeping quiet. Everyone else seemed cheerfully confident that the coming of the Champion meant certain victory, although nobody seemed very clear about how that victory was to come about.

Blade was able to do a few useful things. He started regular firing practice and inspection of weapons among the musketeers. He organized mobile reserves of cavalry, infantry riding in carts, and horse-drawn artillery. He did a good many other things that would improve the odds if the Raufi attacked the city's walls. What he couldn't do was anything that would make the Raufi launch their attack. That, as Mirdon said, would take a miracle.

While Blade was at work as a general, Katerina was working even harder on her "intelligence" assignment—watching Jormin and finding out what he might be up to. Either she was having no luck, or she was being very closemouthed about what she was learning. She would vanish for the better part of a day, then return, obviously exhausted, but unwilling to say anything about where she'd been or what she'd done.

Blade wasn't worried about betrayal now. What bothered him was that something was making Katerina violate one of the first principles of intelligence work:—pass on what you learn as fast as you learn it. If she vanished now, whatever she might have learned about Jormin would vanish with her.

The thought of her vanishing and dying unpleasantly made him uncomfortable. Being uncomfortable about that made him feel even worse. He could not afford to care as much about Katerina's safety as he was doing, or to let her mean as much to him as she had come to. If he went much farther down that road, she would see what was happening to him. Then, if she was still a clear-headed professional, she would find some way to take advantage of what Blade felt. He would not yet call what he felt "love." But by any name it was not what he should be feeling, and it had him more and more worried as the days went by.

Then Katerina vanished for two solid days, and when she returned this time Blade knew where he and everyone else stood.

She came back at dawn. Blade was sitting in an armchair by the empty bed. Sometimes he looked at the bed, more often he sipped from a large cup of spiced brandy on the table by the bed. He realized that he was beginning to drink more than he should. From past experience he knew this meant he was trying to hide from himself the fact that he was under a particularly intense strain.

He drank again and saw that outside the window the sky was turning pale. The campfires of the Raufi no longer shone so brightly in the darkness.

A faint knocking on the door made him start. It was Katerina's signal—a one-two-one combination—but weaker and more uncertain than he'd ever heard it. He put down his cup, picked up the sword leaning against his chair, went to the door and opened it. Katerina nearly collapsed into Blade's arms. He held her out at arm's length for a moment, and his eyes widened in surprise as he saw her clearly.

Her hair was a tangled mess. A large chunk of it was missing on one side, hauled out by the roots. One eye was swollen half-shut. Both cheeks, one ear, and the side of her neck showed deep purple bruises. Along the jawline was a swollen, red patch that looked like the burn from a hot iron. Her lips were bruised and swollen so that he could barely make out any of the words she was murmuring.

"Jormin hopes—with Jade Masters—let in Raufi," was all he caught.

After that Blade stopped listening. He realized Katerina had found what she was looking for—Jormin's plans. He also realized that she'd paid a particularly horrible price for the information. She'd submitted to the demands of a sadistic madman and had barely escaped with her life. Now he understood why she'd been unwilling to talk about her work.

Blade stripped off Katerina's clothes and put her to bed. The rest of her body was as bad as her face, or worse. Whip marks, burns, bruises—there wasn't anything that Jormin's twisted ingenuity had left out.

It seemed rather a pity that Jormin would have to die quickly. At that moment Blade would quite cheerfully have inflicted on the Second Consecrated everything he'd inflicted on Katerina, and much more besides. He found himself picking up a heavy-barreled musket from the corner, gripping it, and bending it slowly but steadily into a complete circle.

Then Blade's head cleared, his rage faded, and he went to work. He called two of the servants, sending one for a doctor and another for Tyan. He summoned a soldier and sent him off to Mirdon. He got out a map of Kano and a roster of the army and began making plans.

Katerina was asleep now. Occasionally she whimpered, little sounds, painfully weak and helpless. After a little while one battered hand—two of the nails were missing—crept out from under the blankets. Blade took it gently and felt it squeeze his, clinging with desperate strength.

He was sitting like that, her hand in his, when the doctor arrived.

The next morning Blade and Katerina sat down to confer with Tyan and Mirdon.

Jormin's plan was simple, according to Katerina. The Jade Masters would lend the Second Consecrated a dozen strong workmen and a dozen good fighters. He would lead all of them to a point on the outer wall where an old drainage tunnel had been blocked off after the building of the Gardens of Stam. The workers would take out the brickwork at either end of the tunnel while the fighters stood guard. Everyone would be properly disguised, with forged passes and everything else necessary. The resources of the Jade Masters would make all that easy.

Once the tunnel was open, fifty Raufi concealed just outside the wall would slip through it. With surprise on their side, they could easily capture the Eighth Gate, only two hundred yards away.

Then two thousand mounted Raufi would charge in. Some would spread out through the Gardens of Stam, sowing panic and death among the troops camped there. Others would ride straight to the poorly guarded gates of the inner city and seize them. The whole Raufi army would then launch a general attack, and with luck dawn would see Kano fallen forever. Whether Jormin, the Jade Masters, or Dahrad Bin Saffar would rule over the ruins was not important.

"A good plan," said Mirdon. "Jormin is mad, but he is also cunning. Tyan spoke more truly than he knew when he said that the Champion's woman would lend us wisdom. Without what you have done, Katerina, and the pain you have endured, I doubt if we could have discovered this until too late."

Normally Tyan would have rebuked anyone taking his words for their own use like that. Instead he let Mirdon's remarks pass without comment. Blade looked from the First Consecrated to the Commander and back again. Seen side by side, they looked even more alike than he'd noticed at first.

Blade unfolded his map of the city and pointed out the Eighth Gate. "There's open ground all around for a considerable distance, and level roads. This means we'll have to be careful to hide everyone well. Otherwise Jormin will get wind of our plans and change his. We'll have one chance to trap him and his Raufi allies, and I want to make it a good one."

Blade talked for half an hour, with only minor interruptions. Finally he folded up the map and said, "I think everything is decided now?" Mirdon nodded. "Good. Then with your leave I shall take Katherina back to our chambers. She really shouldn't be out of bed."

"Gods, no," said Mirdon. "Is there any way she can stay out of this affair altogether? I would gladly sacrifice a hundred good men to spare her that."

Katerina shook her head. "I would be ashamed to have a hundred men die to spare me a little danger. Besides, it would do no good even if I was willing. Jormin will be as suspicious as a mouse who smells a cat. If I do not keep my promise to him, he will certainly become even more suspicious. As the Champion has said, we shall have only one chance. We can leave out nothing."

They were back in their own chambers before Blade said anything more.

"Well, Kat." That had become his pet name for her in his own mind. This was the first time he'd used it aloud to her.

"Well what?"

"Do you think there's only a *little* danger in playing bait to lead Jormin into our trap?"

She sighed and shook her head. "No. I am not a fool."

"I didn't think you were. You're—" Blade cut himself off. He had an overpowering impulse to put into words what she was coming to mean to him. He fought it down. Instead he finished, rather lamely, "You're running more risks than I'm happy about. I'll be glad when this is over."

"So will I." Then she took him firmly by the hand and led him to the bed. At first he protested, suggesting they shouldn't try lovemaking now, when all her wounds were fresh and still hurting. She silenced his objections, first with her lips, then with her body. In the end they made love longer and more passionately than ever before. Blade sensed a quality of desperation in Katerina, as though she had a premonition of her own death and was determined to clutch vigorously at life while it lasted.

As Katerina fell asleep curled up beside him, Blade could not keep an odd thought out of his mind. Was *she* coming to care for *him*, and fighting her impulses just as hard as he was his?

That was not only an odd thought. It was a slightly unpleasant one. At this rate they could wind up making each other perfectly miserable, without much chance of saying even a few words to ease the strain!

Blade sighed. He hadn't been in such a damnably awkward predicament with a woman since he was at Oxford. Unfortunately, there was absolutely nothing to be done about it until after the battle, and damned little to be done even then.

Chapter Twenty-Five

The Gardens of Stam were as dark as the belly of Chaos, thought Jormin. He could barely see his own men following him toward the outer wall. That darkness was a favor from the gods, though. It would be just as hard for anyone to see him and the men.

The soldiers were no more alert than usual tonight, either. They'd challenged the little party only once. Even then the forged pass got it through without any delay or awkward questions.

The party left the graveled path and slipped across smooth, damp grass toward the base of the wall. Jormin sighted the large *kaso* tree that was the most important marker. He paced off twenty steps on a line with the tree, then turned toward the wall. He could see it now— a faint discoloration in the great earth mound where the tunnel had once bored through it. He nodded to the workmen. They scurried forward with their picks and shovels and pry bars and went to work. The Jade Masters' guards spread out in a half-circle, hands on swords. They all had muskets as well, but Jormin's orders were strict—no shooting until the Raufi joined them.

Katerina came up to stand beside Jormin. She wore a plain white robe belted in at the waist, and Jormin knew she wore nothing under it. The thought made him grin.

He noticed that she was wearing a short sword slung on her belt. "You are armed," he whispered. "Why?"

"I could not be sure that you would meet me on time. I had to be ready to protect myself if some drunken soldier came along."

"Ah. I understand." She could not be planning treachery, or even thinking of it. He was certain of that. She was too hungry for what he and he alone could give, what he had already given her. She would do her best to see that nothing went wrong. He could rely on her now and for always, even when they sat together in the High Chamber of the House of the Consecrated and ordered out the victims for public execution!

The workmen were making entirely too much noise for Jormin's peace of mind. He winced at every thud of a falling brick or clink of a tool. The inner end of the tunnel was open now, wide enough for a man to pass through. Jormin saw the workers dropping down into the ditch one by one and squeezing through the hole in the brickwork. Several of the guards followed them. The men could work faster at the outer end of the tunnel. They would be well underground and in less danger of being overheard, thank the gods for that! Jormin licked dry lips and squeezed Katerina's hand, his nails digging into her palms until he heard a little whimper of satisfied pain.

How long he and the remaining guards waited, Jormin couldn't even guess. He only knew that no one came by, no one challenged them, no one seemed to notice that anything unusual was going on. He also knew that the waiting eventually came to an end. First the workmen came scurrying out of the hole, fast enough to scrape skin and tear clothing on jagged edges of brick. Then the guards followed, moving just as fast, their swords sheathed. Jormin stepped forward, ready to rebuke them for their nervousness and wondering what was bothering them.

Then the answer to his question climbed out of the hole, with the first of the Raufi behind him. Like the rest of his men the leader wore a black robe and black sandals. Even his weapons were blackened so that they reflected no light. His hood was shoved back on his head, revealing a high forehead and a hard, bony face, with restless, seeking eyes and an aggressively hooked nose. The chin was concealed behind an unmistakable spade beard.

It was Dahrad Bin Saffar, supreme war chief of the Raufi, come to personally lead his men in the stroke that would destroy Kano forever.

In the room at the top of the western tower of the Eighth Gate Blade paced restlessly back and forth. He could not pace very far. The room was packed with more than forty armed men and all their weapons, as well as a mass of ropes and rope ladders. The room was dark and stifling, because all the shutters were closed and locked to keep any light or sound from escaping. The air was heavy with the smells of leather, oiled metal, and human sweat.

Eventually Blade forced himself to sit down. It was his plan, and he ought to at least look as if he had complete confidence in it! Otherwise, he would end up making all the men following him nervous, from Mirdon on down. He mentally ran over the trap they were setting for Jormin again. He couldn't think of anything he'd left out, or anything the Raufi could do he didn't have some way to meet. Now if they could only go into action at the right time—

Footsteps sounded on the spiral stairs in one corner of the tower. A helmeted head popped up into the room. "Just got the word. They're inside and coming this way."

"Good," said Blade. "How many?"

"Oh, sixty, they guess, lord."

Blade nodded and the head disappeared. Men began tightening sword belts, loading muskets and pistols, tying extra knots in their climbing ropes.

Sixty men. That would be Jormin's crew, plus the

Raufi. There were forty men in the top room of each of the gate towers. That should be enough.

Dahrad Bin Saffar had a high reputation for courtliness and poetic skill with words. These were gifts the Raufi valued, and they honored him more highly because of them.

Tonight, though, he was neither courtly nor poetic. He sharply gestured the kneeling Jormin to rise.

"Are your men all here?"

"Yes, Noble B—"

"Any sign of extra guards?"

"None."

"Good. We will do what we have planned. Take the lead, Jormin."

They headed toward the Eighth Gate at a swift, silent trot. Jormin kept wanting to break into a run, but each time his feet quickened, he heard a voice behind him.

"Slower, man, slower. Hurry, hurry has no blessing from Jannah, and the noise hurry causes still less." They covered the two hundred yards to the Eighth Gate in only a few minutes, although to Jormin it seemed more like a few hours.

The Raufi went swiftly into action. Dahrad must have rehearsed each man over and over again until he could do his part blindfolded. Some fanned out into the Gardens of Stam, to lie in wait with pistols and swords for anyone who might come to interrupt the party. Others began climbing the vines that grew up the inside of the wall, knives in their teeth, to deal with the men mounting guard on top. Still others waited under cover, ready to storm into the towers themselves as soon as the alarm was given. Then they would open the gates, and that would be the signal for the waiting Raufi to come thundering in.

Jormin hoped everything would go well. He badly wanted those two thousand Raufi around him, between him and the vengeance of the Kanoans. He looked at Katerina. She was nervously trying to look in all directions at once and fingering the hilt of her sword. She had even more reason than he did for wanting protection. *She* was not only betraying Kano, she was betraying the Champion of the Gods. The penalty for that would be horrible.

A faint, choked cry sounded high above. Then something sailed through the air and landed with a thud almost at Jormin's feet. It was the body of a soldier from the walls, throat slit from ear to ear. Jormin noticed, with an uneasiness in his stomach, that the man had also been castrated. He looked upward and saw the heads of three Raufi appearing over the railing on top of the wall.

The, from the very top of the western tower, orange flame stabbed out as a light cannon went off. Two of the Raufi on the wall flew high into the air, shredded into bloody rags by a blast of grapeshot. The third lurched, toppled over the railing, and struck the ground almost beside Jormin. His head wasn't human any more, it was a smashed mess of bone and brains.

Jormin went on looking upward because he couldn't do anything else. Sheer terror was freezing every one of his muscles and joints. So he saw clearly the shutters in the windows high in the two towers of the Eighth Gate fly open. He saw ropes and ladders snake out of those windows and men come scrambling down those ropes and ladders. Finally he saw the Champion of the Gods himself come sliding down one of those ropes. It seemed to him that the Champion's eyes glowed fiercely red in the darkness, and that a golden light played about his hair. That was the sight that unfroze Jormin's joints and muscles. With a scream of terror he turned to run.

Blade hit the ground as lightly as a cat, then dropped flat, rolling to confuse anybody aiming at him. A bullet whistled over his head and *spannnnggged* off the wall. The Rauf who'd fired dashed in, throwing his useless pistol aside and raising his sword for a slash at Blade.

Blade leaped to his feet, parried the slash with his own sword, then thrust up under the Rauf's jaw with his dagger. The Rauf stiffened as the dagger's point drove upward into his brain. He collapsed.

As Blade jerked his dagger free more cannon shots roared out from the top of the towers. The soldiers left up there were firing light swivel guns at the Raufi lurking in the bushes farther inside the Gardens of Stam.

164

Grapeshot whistling about their ears would keep those Raufi busy.

In the glare from the cannon fire Blade saw Katerina clearly. She stood alone in her white robe, a startling contrast to all the dark-clad figures dashing madly about. Her sword was drawn. As Blade watched, one of the Jade Masters' guards passed too close to her. She shifted to the right and reached out, fingers closing in the man's long hair to drag him to a stop. Before he could move or shout, Katerina's sword sank into his back. One, two, three quick thrusts, then she was pulling the sword free as the man collapsed and lay twitching.

Blade plunged toward Katerina, sheathing his dagger and drawing a pistol as he ran. He dashed up to her and had a moment to throw an arm around her. Then she turned, pulled away from him, and broke into a run, pulling up the skirts of her robe as she ran. Blade saw that she was heading off after Jormin, raised his pistol, and sighted in on the Second Consecrated.

Katerina saw him aiming and screamed out, "No—don't kill him for me! He's mine!"

Katerina's cry made Blade hesitate for a second. That gave Jormin time to stop, snatch a pistol from under his robe, and fire at the white-robed figure rapidly catching up with him.

Blade saw Katerina reel as the bullet struck her. His own pistol crashed out. The Second Consecrated threw up his arms and fell backward onto the ground, a gaping dark hole in his forehead and another in the back of his bald skull.

Blade wouldn't have noticed or cared if the Second Consecrated had turned into a dragon and flown away into the night. All his attention was for Katerina. He ran to her as she sagged forward onto her knees, one hand clamped to the wound under her right breast. As he reached her, she collapsed, rolling onto her side and then onto her back as her strength faded.

"Kat." His throat was suddenly too tight to say anything more.

Katerina tried to speak but could only cough. Blood bubbled up on her lips and trickled out of the corner of her mouth onto the ground. The white robe was stained dark now, from breast on down. Her sword was still in her hand, also dark from point to hilt with the guard's blood.

At least she'd put down one enemy, Blade thought. Then he realized that she was trying to speak again. More blood came out, but this time so did words. Blade strained to hear them.

"I—wanted—to—love you," she said. "I—"

"I wanted to love you too," said Blade. He bent down to kiss her as her lips curved into a smile. The smile slowly froze as he kissed her. By the time Blade stood up, it was frozen forever.

Someone screamed shrilly, seemingly almost in his ear. "Behind you, Champion! It—" The words ended in another scream and the *chup* of a Raufii sword hacking flesh.

Blade whirled, in time to see a tall bareheaded Rauf charging at him whirling a blood-dripping sword around his head. Blade had heard enough descriptions of Dahrad Bin Saffar to recognize the man he faced. He gave a terrible shout. Here was a miracle indeed! Dahrad Bin Saffar, chief and guiding genius of all the Raufi, delivered into the hands of his enemies for the slaughter!

A moment later Blade wasn't quite sure who was going to be slaughtering whom. Dahrad's sword whistled down at him. He had to jump back to avoid being split down the middle before he could even draw his own sword. Blade drew the sword with one hand and his second pistol with the other. He parried another whistling slash as he raised the pistol. This wasn't the time or place for meeting Dahrad Bin Saffar chivalrously or gallantly, sword against sword. This was the time and place for killing him.

Dahrad saw Blade's raised pistol and shifted his next slash. It missed Blade entirely but smashed across the pistol's barrel with a tremendous clang. Blade's arm flew up as his finger closed on the trigger. The pistol went off with a crash, but the bullet whistled off harmlessly into the darkness. Blade dropped the pistol and went to work with his sword.

Blade was taller than the chief of the Raufi and had a longer reach. But Dahrad Bin Saffar was just as good a fighter and he was wielding a longer and heavier sword.

After the first few slashes and parries Blade knew that he had a first-class opponent on his hands.

Around him Raufi, Jade Masters, and the soldiers of Kano under Mirdon's command were engaged in a wild, swirling, totally chaotic fight, without plan or pattern. Blade heard muskets and pistols going off in ones and twos and ragged volleys, the raspings and clangs of swords on armor, men shouting and screaming. He hadn't heard the sound of the Eighth Gate going up, and that could be either good or bad news. It was good that the Raufi hadn't taken the towers and opened the gate. It was bad that Mirdon hadn't beaten back the Raufi enough to open the gate himself and let the enemy's riders into the trap prepared for them.

Dahrad's sword whistled over Blade's head close enough to scrape his helmet. Blade got home a thrust of his own, but it didn't push through the coat of fine mail Dahrad wore under his robe. It wouldn't matter whether the gate opened or not if Dahrad Bin Saffar cut him in two first! Blade settled down to concentrate grimly on the opponent at hand.

The duel went on as the two men stamped around and around each other, slashing and thrusting, sparks flying as their swords met and sweat pouring off both of them. Blade kept looking for something to give him an edge. He couldn't spend all night fighting with the Raufi chief! But every time he thought he'd found an opening, Dahrad was blocking him or fading out of reach. Fortunately, Blade was able to do the same.

The duel went on, and Blade began to wonder if it *would* go on all night, whether he could afford this or not. Dahrad Bin Saffar was striking harder and faster now. It seemed that being able to hold on so well against Blade was filling him with more confidence, more aggressiveness. His sword smashed down against Blade's until each impact jarred Blade from head to foot and made his sword vibrate like an iron rod hammered on by a blacksmith.

Dahrad launched an overhead slash, the strongest attack yet. Blade's sword leaped up to block it. Dahrad's sword smashed down against Blade's, hard up against the crossbar of the hilt. With a sharp metallic *crannnng*, Blade's sword broke off at the hilt.

Dahrad's furious slash sent his heavy sword whistling on down, until its edge sank deep into the ground. Blade dropped his useless sword hilt and closed in. His booted foot came down on Dahrad's sword faster than the man could raise it. For a moment the sword was immobilized Blade pivoted and kicked out hard with his other foot. Dahrad Bin Saffar sprang back, just in time to keep Blade's foot from smashing his jaw to a ruin. As he sprang back, he let go of his sword

Blade swung down out of his pivot and snatched the fallen sword from the ground. He swung it three times about his head, so fast that it hissed and whistled. Then he charged in at Dahrad Bin Saffar. The Rauf stood as if he had one foot caught in a trap. He seemed paralyzed by the spectacle of his own sword coming at him in the hands of an enemy.

Blade swung the sword three more times. Dahrad Bin Saffar drew a dagger, but the first swing of Blade's sword knocked the dagger out of the man's hand and sent it flying. The second swing chopped deeply into his thigh, and his lips curled back from his white teeth in a defiant snarl. The third swing slashed clear through Dahrad's neck, and his head flew ten feet and rolled along the ground. The spouting body collapsed backward as Blade dashed to retrieve the head before any of Dahrad's tribesmen could rescue it. When he picked it up by the beard, the snarl was still frozen there on the lifeless face.

As Blade stood there, holding Dahrad Bin Saffar's head, he heard the rumble and squeal of the gate opening. He whirled as someone shouted his name and saw Mirdon running toward him.

"Champion! Champion! We have the edge on them, and I have ordered the gate opened. We must get back into the tower, or—" He broke off and stopped abruptly as Blade held out his grisly trophy.

"Gods above!" exploded Mirdon. "Him!" He shook his head in a daze. "A second miracle has come indeed! You—you killed him?"

Blade nodded. "I also killed Jormin, after he killed Katerina."

"Ka—" began Mirdon, even more dazed and bewildered. Blade didn't wait for the Commander to organize his thoughts. He tossed Dahrad's bleeding head to Mirdon, saw him catch it, then turned and ran toward where Katerina's body lay. He knew the kind of battle that would be sweeping through this area in a few minutes. He didn't want to leave Katerina's body lying in the middle of that battle, where it would be trampled and mangled.

As he reached Katerina, the roar of Raufi drums and the blare of their trumpets sounded outside the walls. The two thousand mounted men were on their way toward the open gate. Blade lifted the body in his arms and ran back the way he'd come, toward the door of the stairs in the western tower of the Eighth Gate. As he started to run, he heard the rumble of wheels and the pounding of hooves from the direction of the Garden of Stam. The mobile reserve was moving into position. The trap for the oncoming riders was being set, and in a few minutes more it would be sprung.

Blade ran as he'd seldom run in his life, leaping over fallen weapons, skirting fallen bodies. Most of the fallen lay still. Some were still writhing feebly. He couldn't stop for any of them, friend or foe. He could only plunge forward, arms locked tightly around Katerina, holding her body as tightly as he'd ever held the live, warm, loving woman.

He plunged forward until the door gaped dark before him. Two of the soldiers were still on guard with muskets held ready. They let him through, then dashed in after him, slamming and barring the ironbound door behind them. Just as the door cut off the outside world, Blade heard the swelling rumble of the Raufi as they began moving in toward the wall.

Blade ran up the winding stairs of the tower even faster than he'd run across the level ground. His chest was heaving as he burst out into the open air on top of the tower. He laid Katerina gently on the stones, then turned to the nearest soldier.

"Do you have—"

A volley of shots sounded from outside the walls, rising above the swelling sound of the approaching riders. Bullets whistled overhead and spattered on the stones. Soldiers all around Blade threw themselves flat on their stomachs. Only Blade continued to stand, looking out over the desert as the Raufi charged in toward the wall.

They fired more shots as they came in, without shooting at anyone or anything in particular. They seemed to be shooting for the fun of it, out of high spirits, as they rode in toward the open gate that marked the way into Kano and certain victory.

Well outside the walls the Raufi slowed down. Drums roared again and trumpets called out as the two thousand riders sorted themselves into a column narrow enough to pass through the gate. Then they were on the move again, at a trot, a canter, a gallop. They pounded up to the wall, vanished into the gate, and emerged on the other side in the Gardens of Stam. Blade rushed to the inner side of the tower. All around him the soldiers sprang to their feet and followed him, desperately reloading their muskets and pistols, winding up their crossbows, shouting and cheering. They shouldn't be making so much noise, Blade thought. But the Raufi were making so much more noise that ten times as many soldiers couldn't have made themselves heard.

Then came a sound that drowned out soldiers, Raufi, and everything else. The trap closed. Twelve heavy cannon crammed to the muzzle with grapeshot let fly at the Raufi. Three hundred iron balls swept down the column. Blade saw human heads and arms fly high into the air, saw bodies drop from the saddle cut completely in half, saw camels fall to the ground with all four legs blown off in a single moment. The echoing roar of the cannon died away, and a pandemonium of human and animal screams replaced it.

The soldiers around Blade stopped cheering long enough to lean over the wall and fire their muskets and crossbows. Then they drew back to reload. The twelve cannon fired again.

The Raufi were still coming. Some of them were simply pushed on through the gate by the pressure of their comrades behind them. Others seemed to have hopes of riding down the guns and seeping out into the Gardens of Stam. They were waving their swords and firing off pistols as they rode in through the gate.

A dozen more guns roared out on the right flank, lighter guns firing loads of musket balls. The new line of Raufi did not die as spectacularly as the first, but they died just as fast. Riderless camels charged about wildly, swerving as they trod on writhing bodies, screaming with the pain of wounds.

Both batteries of guns fired again. Then Kanoan trumpets sounded for the first time that night, and five hundred horsemen swept in from the left. They wasted no time firing, but charged home with sword and lance. A good many of them couldn't stay in their saddles and fell, to be trampled to death under the hooves of their comrades' horses. A good many more missed their blows. A solid mass remained to crash into the Raufi at a full gallop, taking them in the rear, cutting their column in two.

As the surviving Raufi tried to rally and fight their way back through to the gate and out of Kano, musketeers came running out from behind trees. They dashed into accurate range, fired, then dropped their muskets and set to with swords. Behind them ran the gunners from the artillery, waving axes, rammers, handspikes, and the other tools of their trade.

Nobody could hope to sort out who was doing what to whom in that shambles. Even the soldiers around Blade stopped firing, afraid of hitting friend instead of enemy. Nobody could hope to know how long it went on, either.

Eventually it all came to an end, and that was enough for Blade. The battle was over. Jormin, Dahrad Bin Saffar, and most of the two thousand Raufi would never trouble Kano or the Kanoans again. He spread a cloth over Katerina's face, then left her lying where he'd put her and went down the tower stairs to the ground.

A wide area around the Eighth Gate was a ploughed-up, hoof-marked shambles. Dying men and animals, bodies, parts of bodies, pools of blood, and smashed or discarded weapons were everywhere. A continuous low moaning rose from the maimed and dying, and the equally inescapable reek of death rose from the rest. In the Gardens all around the battlefield, large trees stood stripped of leaves, smaller trees lay chopped completely through, bushes and flowerbeds lay where they had been violently uprooted or trampled flat.

Silence had almost returned when Blade saw Mirdon

riding toward him on a borrowed cavalry horse. The Commander carried nothing but a bare sword and a bloodstained cloth bag, and in his eyes was a look Blade didn't like very much. He remembered the night he and Mirdon had first met, when the Commander had spurred his horse up an impossibly steep slope to get at Blade. That night Mirdon had had the face of a man determined to do the impossible or die trying. Now the same look was there, even stronger.

"Ho, Champion!" shouted Mirdon. "Will you ride with me?"

"Where to?"

"I ride to throw Dahrad's head—" he held up the sack "—in the faces of the whole of the Raufi. We have already accomplished tonight most of the miracle we needed. But our work will not be finished until we have made the Raufi storm the walls in the face of our guns and our courage."

"Won't what we've done already be enough?" said Blade.

"Perhaps it could be," said Mirdon. "But the hope of Kano must not rely on a 'perhaps.' It must rely on what is certain. Not unless I hurl Dahrad Bin Saffar's head into the very camp of the Raufi will it be certain they will come against our walls. Then they will come, and we will have our victory and our vengeance."

Blade found he did not care as much as he perhaps ought to for the vengeance of the Kanoans. But he knew one thing for certain. If Mirdon was going to ride out on this mad mission, it was his place as the Champion of the Gods to ride along with the Commander. He certainly had no hope of persuading Mirdon *not* to ride.

"Very well, Mirdon," he said. "Find me a horse. Let us ride out."

It took a few minutes to find a horse able to carry Blade's two hundred and some pounds without strain. Then Blade and Mirdon rode out of the Eighth Gate at a canter. The soldiers lined the wall and the tops of the towers to watch them go. Doubtless they thought both men were riding to certain death. But mortals do not question a Champion of the Gods, and the soldiers of Kano had long since given up trying to argue with Mirdon when he had his mind made up.

They cantered past a few stray Raufi wandering about on foot, too stunned by their defeat to pay any attention to the riders or even find their way back to their own lines. They cantered past more bodies of men and camels. Then they were out into the open and the city was receding into the darkness behind them.

Here there had been miles of trees, bushes, and gardens before the Raufi came. Now everything living had been trampled out of existence, shot to splinters, or chopped up to feed the Raufi campfires. The ground was bare and hard, and it stretched for two open, level miles to the Raufi lines. Mirdon dug in his spurs, and his horse bounded forward at a gallop. Blade followed.

A full moon was up by now. It gave the ground underfoot and the dust the horses kicked up a luminous quality. It seemed to Blade that they weren't riding so much as flying effortlessly over a great expanse of pure, glowing light. He began to have the feeling that there were no Raufi ahead, that this flight would go on forever, to the end of the world and whatever might lie beyond it. The pounding of the horses' hooves on the hard ground faded out of Blade's senses, the ruined and splintered trees faded, Mirdon himself faded.

A volley of bullets whistling past snapped Blade abruptly back to reality. Three hundred yards off to the right, more than a hundred mounted Raufi were angling in toward the two riders. Blade looked ahead and saw a line of campfires stretching clear across their path in a wide arc. Mirdon did not pull rein or show any sign he'd seen anything. The two riders plunged on toward the campfires. More bullets whistled past, closer this time.

Blade was just about to shout to Mirdon when the Commander himself seemed to wake from his daze. His sword flashed in the moonlight as he whirled it high over his head. He swung his horse around toward the mounted Raufi.

Blade also pulled his horse around, considerably relieved. He would have followed Mirdon wherever the Commander had led him taking any risks involved. As Champion of the Gods, he had no choice. But he could hardly regret not having to commit suicide!

Somehow, Mirdon was managing to get still more

speed out of his horse as they charged toward the Raufi. Blade found it hard not to fall behind. The thunder of hooves and the rank sweat of the laboring horses rose to fill the night and shut out the rest of the world. Now it seemed that they weren't just flying across the ground. It seemed to Blade that they might fly up and away into the sky.

They came up to the Raufi with bullets whistling about their ears, kicking up dust all around their horses, but not hitting them. The darkness and the battle and the strangeness of everything seemed to be unnerving the enemy and throwing off their aim.

The two rode straight in until Blade felt that he could practically reach out and touch the leading Rauf. He saw Mirdon drop the reins and reach down for the canvas bag that swung from his saddle. He saw Mirdon's arm whip out and over, hurling the bag out at the Raufi. He saw the Raufi scatter, spurring their camels frantically in all directions, some of them falling out of their saddles. Mirdon gave a great whooping roar of laughter at the spectacle the Raufi were making of themselves. Then a musket crashed out, and he reeled in the saddle as the bullet took him under his raised sword arm.

Mirdon's horse felt the rider's hand slacken on the reins, and it began to slow. Blade knew that in another moment it might panic and bolt, or hurl Mirdon helplessly to the ground. He frantically urged his own horse forward until he was riding alongside Mirdon. The Commander's face had gone as white as flour. Blood trickled from the corner of his mouth and pumped steadily from his wound.

Mirdon's arm drooped and his sword fell to the ground. Blade dropped his reins and guided his horse with his knees as he reached out for Mirdon. The Commander lurched and practically fell into Blade's outstretched arms. Blade gave one tremendous heave and Mirdon seemed to fly out of his saddle. He nearly flew right over Blade's horse and pulled Blade to the ground with him, but somehow Blade caught him. With the last of his strength Mirdon twisted himself into a sitting position in front of Blade. Then his head lolled back against Blade's shoulder, and his mouth opened in a gush of blood. Blade hauled his horse's head around toward the walls of Kano and dug in his spurs again.

The horse had less than half its strength left, and it was carrying nearly twice as much weight as before. Somehow Blade's spurs and curses pushed the horse along at a lumbering trot until they were out of range of the enemy. Then the horse slowed to a walk, and nothing Blade could do would push it along any faster. It didn't matter now, though. A squadron of cavalry and a couple of light guns came out from the Eighth Gate and escorted them in.

As they rode in through the gate, Blade heard the First Consecrated's trumpeters sound a long blast. So he was not surprised to see Tyan himself waiting just inside the gate. His sedan chair with its slave bearers stood behind him. Beside it stood two blue-draped litters. Blue, Blade recalled, was the color of mourning in Kano.

There were plenty of hands to lift Mirdon's body down off the horse. That was all anybody could do for him now. Without any orders, half a dozen soldiers carried the body over to one of the litters. Tyan himself bent over it, closed Mirdon's eyes, and drew one end of the draperies over his face.

The tension was draining out of Blade now. He saw a white-robed form stretched out on the other litter—Katerina. Slowly he walked over to stand beside Tyan. Their eyes met for a moment, in a wordless understanding that somehow said a great deal without saying anything Blade could grasp clearly. Blade noticed that there were tears in Tyan's eyes. Then, side by side, they followed the litters as the soldiers bore them off.

Chapter Twenty-Six

Whatever Tyan let himself feel at night, he was all business and grim determination by dawn.

"This may or may not be the end of the Raufi," he told Blade over breakfast. "For all that Mirdon has done, that is still in the hands of the gods. But most certainly this shall mean the end of the Jade Masters. That is altogether in our hands, and our hands will be swift and just."

Strong bands of soldiers and armed civilians scoured Kano all day, rounding up the families of every man known to be a Jade Master or one of their servants. The families were crammed roughly into the prison tower. Then Tyan called the Jade Masters, their chief craftsmen, their stewards, and the officers of their guards to the House of the Consecrated. Blade was there in full armor when Tyan delivered his message.

Tyan wasted no words. "The Jade Masters stand guilty of treason to Kano. By the laws of this city, by the laws of the gods, by common human wisdom you deserve to die. Yet many of you are fighters, which Kano needs. If you live and fight through the days ahead, you may yet be forgiven.

"I do not trust you, however, to fight merely in the hope of forgiveness. So I have taken your wives and children. I shall keep them until the fate of Kano is settled.

"If any among you prove treacherous again, your families will die. If the Raufi storm the city, your families will die. But if you go to the walls and help beat back the Raufi, your families will live, whether you do or not."

Once more, Blade was glad that good luck and good management had made the First Consecrated Tyan of Kano his friend instead of his enemy. As an enemy, that old man could have been more dangerous than the Raufi, Jormin, Geddo, Stul, and the Gudki all put together. As a friend, Tyan had done everything Blade could have hoped for. Tyan hadn't saved Katerina, but that was simply wretchedly bad luck. Katerina had died the way she must have expected to die when she had entered her chosen profession—that is, violently, and before her time. She had not died before knowing the happiness of caring and being cared for, and that was something she probably hadn't expected.

In any case, Blade did not have much time to mourn Katerina. Two days later, the Raufi attacked the walls of Kano with all their strength.

It was not a battle that day, it was a massacre. The Raufi came against intact walls manned by soldiers inspired by the Champion of the Gods and determined to revenge the Champion's slain woman and Commander Mirdon. Aiding the soldiers were the fighters of the Jade Masters, more frightened for their families than for themselves, and many thousands of eager and determined civilians of all ages and both sexes. The Raufi were mad with rage at the death of their great war chief, but their rage didn't help them. As Mirdon had planned, it simply drove them on to an even worse defeat than they could have suffered otherwise.

Afterward Blade couldn't recall that he'd ever been in a great battle where he had so little to do. He and Tyan spent the day in the Gardens of Stam, encouraging the fighters and giving occasional orders. Blade only had his sword out of its scabbard once, when a handful of Raufi managed to get into the Gardens.

The battle went on all day, with no quarter given or asked for. By sunset there were no more Raufi attacks, because there were hardly any more Raufi. Dahrad Bin Saffar led close to fifty thousand warriors out of the desert against the city. Less than ten thousand rode away. It would be generations before the Raufi could again threaten Kano. It would probably be centuries before they would want to try.

In Tyan's private chambers everything was as silent as ever. Outside in the street, there was noisy rejoicing at the victory and equally noisy mourning for the dead. Not a sound crept through the massive walls of the House of the Consecrated. Nothing disturbed the First Consecrated and the Champion of the Gods as they sat across the table from each other. On the table between them lay the great jeweled staff of the First Consecrated.

When the last servant had vanished, Tyan raised his wine cup.

"To Kano."

"To Kano," replied Blade. He added as he drank, "A city with a future."

"A future it owes to you," said Tyan.

Blade shrugged. "Perhaps. Also much to Katerina and Mirdon."

There was a long silence. Then Tyan spoke quietly. "Mirdon was my son, Champion. Against all the laws and customs that bind the Consecrated, I was the father

177

of a son. So I think I can say that I feel with you in what you have lost."

Blade nodded without speaking. He couldn't think of any response that needed putting into words. Tyan had explained much and offered sympathy. What more was necessary? He drank again, emptying his cup, then poured more wine from the silver jug.

Another long silence. Then Tyan heaved a sigh. With an almost visible effort, he set aside his memories and smiled his usual thin smile.

"Champion, I promised when we first began this game that I would one day ask *how* you escaped from the Mouth of the Gods. You are certainly a warrior such as neither the Raufi nor Kano have known since the days of ancient legend. It is just as certain that the ritual of sacrifice is designed so that *no one* can escape as you did, except by a greater miracle than we have seen these past few days. How did you do it, Champion?"

"I—Tyan, will there be any danger to anyone if I tell you?"

"Well, if it turns out that there was weakness or corruption among the servants of the Consecrated—" He broke off. "No, I will give you my word. No one shall suffer, regardless of what you tell me."

Blade nodded. He'd gained a few seconds to think by his delaying tactics. Now he would have to give the alarmingly shrewd Tyan a convincing natural explanation of an escape that indeed had been a miracle! He shook his head and absent-mindedly reached out to lay a hand on the great staff of office.

Before Tyan could rebuke him or he could say a word, Blade felt a faint dart of pain in his head. He started to rise, his hand still on the staff. The pain came again, three times in rapid succession, each time stronger. Blade sat back down again, a great sense of relief welling up in him. The computer had reached out to his brain again and had gripped it. This time there was no one he needed to help. This time he would be going back Home, back to London, away from this nightmare in Dimensions. He did not know how he knew this. He only knew that it would be so.

The pain roared and thundered. Blade staggered to his feet, both hands now clutching the great staff. Across the table he could see Tyan leaping up so fast that his chair went over backward, eyes staring in total disbelief. The First Consecrated's mouth was open, but Blade could no longer hear anything except the roaring in his own head. Then the chamber started fading before his eyes. The last thing he saw as it faded out was Tyan throwing himself facedown on the floor, hands toward Blade and lips moving frantically. Curses, prayers, what? Blade didn't know, and he would never know.

The chamber vanished, and Blade was on his horse again, riding across the moonlit land toward the Raufi, clutching the great staff. Underfoot there was nothing but moonlight, and the horse struck silver sparks as it galloped.

Another horse was galloping beside him, but it was not Mirdon who rode it now. It was Katerina, naked, with a sword in her hand. She reached out with the sword toward Blade, and Blade stretched out his free hand to grasp the tip of the sword.

The air glowed and sparked between his fingers and the sword. Golden fire burst out into tiny balls that sailed away on the wind, then swelled upward. It swelled up until the flames reached out toward Blade and blotted out his view of Katerina. Fire went on swelling until there was nothing around him except the swirling golden fire.

Then the fire was gone, and in its place a great blackness that swallowed him up between one heartbeat and the next.

Chapter Twenty-Seven

Several people were not particularly happy after Blade returned to Home Dimension.

Lord Leighton and J sat in the living room of J's London flat. J found himself extremely tempted to just go on sitting there, until cobwebs formed over him or at least until the maid came around in the morning to clean up the room. He suspected that Lord Leighton felt exactly the same way. He'd never seen the scientist look so red-eyed, haggard, and generally wretched after the conclusion of one of Blade's trips into Dimension X.

Well, it was hard to blame the man. He himself didn't feel much better. It was absolutely maddening to consider what had happened—and it was also slightly chilling to consider what *might* have happened. They'd found a method of passing two people at once from one Dimension to another. They'd found another person fully equal to Blade in her ability to enter Dimension X and survive. They'd lost her, too, but however maddening that was, it was the luck of battle. It would have been almost as awkward to have her back as it had been to lose her with much of the information she could have provided! Katerina *had* lived, she *had* survived in Dimension X, and in doing so she'd proved conclusively that Blade was not unique. Somewhere in the world there were other people who could survive the trip into Dimension X. The problem, though, was *finding* them. There nothing was new, nothing was changed. The long search would become longer still, and there was no helping it.

The "might have beens" were even more unsettling, even if none of them had happened. There were so many of them that it was impossible to describe them, or even to count them all. But the total added up to one conclusion—this time they had come closer to losing Blade than ever before. They hadn't lost him, but that was because their luck—and Blade's—hadn't run out. A dozen unknown factors had been thrown into the whole affair, and that none of them had killed Blade or trapped him forever in Dimension X was as big a miracle as Kano's defeat of the Raufi!

Leighton, of course, was feeling particularly bad because he was responsible for some of these unknowns, without being able to say a word to explain any of them! He felt he was failing in his duties to the Project, to Richard Blade, and to his own reputation as a scientist. Which of the three failures preyed on his mind the most was impossible to tell. But J was quite sure that they added up to a grisly burden. For once he felt totally sympathetic toward the scientist, and he made a mental promise to do everything he could to help Leighton. The man was past eighty, close to the end of his life and career, and here his greatest achievement, the Project, had turned around and bitten him!

At least, J added mentally, he would do everything to help Leighton that wouldn't endanger Richard Blade.

Meanwhile, there was a decision to be made. Push on with the next mission, or defer it until—until what? That was the question. Blade was in fine shape physically and mentally, although he was certainly angry, and he seemed somewhat depressed about something he hadn't mentioned. The two women, Arllona and Katerina, were both dead. There was nothing more to find out from or about either of them. There really wasn't any reason for delaying, except perhaps objections from Richard, and their own nerves. But there wouldn't be any objections from Richard—there never were. And as for their own nerves—well, if they'd given in to those at all, the Project would have come to a halt years ago. This was no time to start.

J rose, went to the sideboard, and brought back the whiskey decanter, the soda water, and two glasses. He prepared two very large whiskies-and-soda and handed one to Leighton.

Leighton did not pick his up. But he did raise his fatigue-reddened eyes and look at J.

"Well, what *do* you think we ought to do?"

"In what sense?"

"Should we defer the next mission, or proceed on schedule?"

J couldn't help laughing. Leighton's mind had been working along the same lines as his.

"Well, what have you concluded?"

"We might as well push on."

J laughed again. For this moment at least, they were two minds with a single thought.

"I quite agree," he said. They raised their glasses and drank.

Richard Blade sat in a West End bar and contemplated ordering another in what was already a long series of whiskies. He finally decided against it. He did not feel particularly good, and from here on drinking would make things worse rather than better.

He'd left something out of his report on the mission,

and he was wondering if he'd been wise to do so. Not what he felt about "being buggered about from Dimension to Dimension like a bloody table-tennis ball"—he'd let them know his feelings on that at great length. He was angry about that, although not really angry *at* anyone, since Leighton himself seemed to be almost completely at sea over what had happened.

What he'd left out was everything about what he and Katerina had felt for each other. For all that J and Lord Leighton knew, the two of them had been an effective partnership of two professionals, allies by necessity. They didn't and they wouldn't know about partnership of two lovers, or about what Blade had felt as he knelt beside the dying Katerina.

He'd loved Katerina, but he'd fought off saying it even to himself until it was too late. He was not proud of that. He couldn't be. So he would never mention that.

He wasn't bothered about having fallen in love with a KGB agent, at least not one who'd been in love with him too. He saw clearly that the very strengths and gifts that had let Katerina travel into Dimension X and survive made her the kind of woman he could love. It hadn't been inevitable that they would fall in love—but there had always been a good chance of it.

Yet could he expect even J to see things that way? J would bend over backwards not to pass any judgments. But, for the first time in his life, Richard Blade had let his professional behavior be affected by a woman. It probably would be the last time, too, but in his profession once could be too often.

No, J should not learn of it, and he would not. It would be a strain never to mention it, but it would not be as much of a strain as any of the alternatives.

Blade decided that he would order another drink after all, to celebrate the decision.

On the outer wall of Kano, Tyan sat and looked out over the land beyond. Smoke rose from the fires where the bodies of the Raufi were being burned, hazing the landscape, but Tyan would not have seen it clearly in any case. His vision, like his thoughts, was on things much farther away.

182

He had played a trick. True, it was a trick to save Kano. But he had played it with one who was indeed the Champion of the Gods, sent by them for the salvation of Kano. The gods had not punished Kano for his trick, and for this he thanked them.

As for himself—well, he was old, Kano was safe, and his son was dead. If the gods chose to exact a price from him for his blasphemy with their champion, then so be it. He would not even pray to avert it.

He would pray, however, that they would do what they wished to do soon. Even as a child, he had never liked waiting. Now he liked it even less.

Tyan sighed, lifted his eyes to the sky, and began to pray.